Wringer

JERRY SPINELLI

Wringer

JOANNA COTLER BOOKS
AN IMPRINT OF HARPERCOLLINSPUBLISHERS

I am grateful to the following for help in writing this story:

Steven and Silvia Hagopian, Tom Reeves, and Laura DeSimone

—J.S.

Wringer

Copyright © 1997 by Jerry Spinelli

For information address HarperCollins Children's Books, a division of
HarperCollins Publishers, 10 East 53rd Street, New York, NY 10022.

Visit our web site at
http://www.harperchildrens.com

Library of Congress Cataloging-in-Publication Data
Spinelli, Jerry.
    Wringer / by Jerry Spinelli.
        p.   cm.
    "Joanna Cotler Books."
    Summary: As Palmer comes of age, he must either accept the violence of being
a wringer at his town's annual Pigeon Day or find the courage to oppose it.
    ISBN 0-06-024913-7. — ISBN 0-06-024914-5 (lib. bdg.)
    [1. Courage—Fiction.   2. Violence—Fiction.   3. Pigeons—Fiction.]   I. Title.
PZ7.S75663Wr   1997   96-37897
[Fic]—dc21   CIP
                                                                                 AC

Typography by Al Cetta
7   8   9   10
❖
First Edition

TO JERRY AND HELEN WEISS

WAYMER—Hundreds of sharpshooters in and around this rural community are cleaning their shotguns as they look forward to Saturday's 63rd annual Pigeon Day. Beginning at around 8 A.M., participants who have paid a fee will each have the chance to shoot at ten to twenty pigeons as they are released from boxes.

Shooters are scored according to a point system that, at day's end, rewards the most accurate of all with the coveted Sharpshooter's trophy. Proceeds from the shoot go to maintain the community's 40-acre park.

Organizers said approximately 5,000 birds are acquired for the event. Some are purchased from local breeders, while others are trapped in big-city railroad yards.

The pigeons are placed in white boxes. Each shooter takes a turn firing at a series of birds as they are released individually by ropes attached to the boxes.

Most birds are downed. Many are killed instantly, some are wounded. All downed birds are retrieved by so-called wringer boys, who break the necks of the wounded and place all bodies in plastic bags. The bodies are then sold for fertilizer. A few birds manage to escape.

The shoot takes place in a festive, picnic atmosphere of barbecued chicken, water ice and frolicking children. Attendance last year was estimated at 4,000.

Pigeon Day is the traditional climax of Family Fest, a weeklong celebration of amusement rides, pie-eating contests . . .

Wringer

1

He did not want to be a wringer.

This was one of the first things he had
learned about himself. He could not have said
exactly when he learned it, but it was very early.
And more than early, it was deep inside. In the
stomach, like hunger.

But different from hunger, different and
worse. Because it was always there. Hunger
came only sometimes, such as just before dinner
or on long rides in the car. Then, quickly, it was
gone the moment it was fed. But this thing,
there was no way to feed it. Well, one way perhaps, but that was unthinkable. So it was never
gone.

In fact, gone was something it could not be,
for he could not escape it any more than he
could escape himself. The best he could do was
forget it. Sometimes he did so, for minutes,
hours, maybe even for a day or two.

But this thing did not like to be forgotten.
Like air escaping a punctured tire, it would

spread out from his stomach and be every-where. Inside and outside, up and down, day and night, just beyond the foot of his bed, in his sock drawer, on the porch steps, at the edges of the lips of other boys, in the sudden flutter from a bush that he had come too close to. Everywhere.

Just to remind him.

This thing, this not wanting to be a wringer, did it ever knock him from his bike? Untie his sneaker lace? Call him a name? Stand up and fight?

No. It did nothing. It was simply, merely there, a whisper of featherwings, reminding him of the moment he dreaded above all others, the moment when the not wanting to be a wringer would turn to becoming one.

In his dreams the moment had already come. In his dreams he looks down to find his hands around the neck of the pigeon. It feels silky. The pigeon's eye is like a polished shirt button. The pigeon's eye is orange with a smaller black button in the center. It looks up at him. It does not blink. It seems as if the bird is about to speak, but it does not. Only the voices speak: "Wring it! Wring it! Wring it!"

He cannot. He cannot wring it, nor can he let go. He wants to let go, desperately, but his fingers are stone. And the voices chant: "Wring it! Wring it!" and the orange eye stares.

Sometimes he wished it would come after him, chase him, this thing he did not want to be. Then at least he could run from it, he could hide. But the thing never moved. It merely waited. Waited for him to come to it.

And he would. He would come to it as surely as nine follows eight and ten follows nine. He would come to it without having to pedal or run or walk or even move a muscle. He would fall smack into the lap of it without doing anything but breathe. In the end he would get there simply by growing one day older.

2

His mother called, "Palmer, hurry. They're coming."

The doorbell rang.

"Palmer!"

He flew down the stairs.

His mother waved him on. "Go, go. It's *your* birthday. *You* invited them."

At the door he turned, suddenly afraid to open it. He did not want to be disappointed. "You sure it's them?"

His mother's eyes rolled. "No, it's my Aunt Millie. Open it."

He opened the door—and there they were! Beans. Mutto. Henry. Three grinning faces. Shoving wrapped gifts into his chest. Storming past him into his house, Beans bellowing, "Where's the grub?"

Palmer stayed in the doorway, fighting back tears. They were tears of relief and joy. He had been sure they would not come. But they did. He wondered if they would give him a nickname. What would it possibly be? But that was asking too much. This was plenty. They were here. With presents! They liked him. He was one of them. At last.

Arms full of gifts, he pushed the door shut with his foot and joined them in the dining room. Beans was scooping chocolate icing from the birthday cake onto his finger. With the drama of a sword-swallower, he threw back his head and sank his finger into his mouth. When it came out, it was clean. Mutto cackled and did likewise. Henry stared at Palmer's mother, who was glaring at Beans.

Palmer's mother did not like Beans. She wasn't crazy about Mutto or Henry either, but she especially did not like Beans. "He's a sneak and a troublemaker," she had said. "He's got a mean streak." And she was right. But he was also leader of all the kids on the street, at least the ones under ten years old. It had always been that way. Beans was boss as surely and naturally as any king who ever sat upon a throne.

"But he's the boss," Palmer would explain to his mother.

"Boss, my foot," she would snort and turn away.

Some things mothers just did not under-stand.

"Open the presents!" Beans barked. He rapped on the table with a spoon. Mutto rapped a spoon also.

Palmer dumped the gifts onto the table and for the first time took a good look at them. They were wrapped in newspaper, sloppily fitted and closed with black tape. No ribbons, no bows, no bright paper.

He tore open the first. It was an apple core, brown and rotting. "It's from me!" piped Mutto. "You like it?" Mutto howled.

Palmer giggled. "It's great. Thanks." What a guy, that Mutto.

The other gifts were a crusty, holey, once-white sock from Henry, and from Beans a thumb-size, brown something that Palmer finally recognized as an ancient cigar butt.

Silverware hopped as Beans and Mutto pounded the dining room table, laughing.

Palmer's mother, still glaring, came with more gifts. These had ribbons and bows and beautiful paper. "Gee," she said, "after those nice presents you just got, I feel really cheesy giving you this junk."

Palmer opened them: a soccer ball, a book, a pair of sneakers, a Monopoly game.

"Thanks, Mom," he said. It was pointless to say more, pointless to say, I like their presents just as much as yours, because they did it themselves. That means something. It means: We came into your house. We gave you a cigar butt. You are one of us.

Palmer's mother lit the candles, nine of them on the chocolate cake with chocolate icing. She started off the "Happy Birthday" song but soon was drowned out by the boys, who screamed it rather than sang. When they came to the line "Happy birthday, dear"—they glanced at each other and belted out—"*Sno-ots!* Happy birthday to you!"

So they had done it after all, given him a nickname. Snots. He moved his tongue silently over the name, feeling its shape.

For a moment he wondered if he would be getting The Treatment, but he pushed that thought aside. He was getting greedy. He had already been blessed enough for one day.

"Make a wish," said his mother, "and blow out the candles."

He stared into the ring of candles—nine

yellow flames, plump and liquidlike, perched on their wicks—and suddenly he felt the old fear, launching itself from his shoulder and brushing a wingtip across his cheek. And just as suddenly it was gone and Beans was croaking, "Hey, we ain't got all day. I got lotsa wishes if you don't." Beans leaned across the table, took a deep breath and blasted away. The flames vanished. Wick tips glowed orange for a second, then turned black.

Let Beans blow away, Palmer didn't care. Nothing could blow out the candleglow he felt inside. Palmer LaRue—Snots—the world's newest nine-year-old—was one of the guys.

3

It was never meant to be a real party. "Just cake and ice cream," Palmer's mother had said, "that's all." She did not want "those little hoodlums," as she called them, in her house any longer than necessary.

The boys dragged out the cake and ice cream as long as they could. Beans and Mutto kept leaving their chairs and wandering around and flopping on furniture. Palmer's mother kept shooing them back to the table.

"I guess you're done now," she said, anxious to shoo them out the door.

"More ice cream," they said.

And then Beans started having to go to the bathroom, or so he said. He made three trips upstairs, probably spying on Palmer's room. As he headed up the stairs for his fourth trip, Palmer's mother grabbed his arm and announced, "Okay, boys, party's over. Time to go out and enjoy the summer sunshine."

As the guys left, Henry surprised Palmer's

mother by saying thank you for the party. "Yeah," Palmer called back, "thanks, Mom."

Palmer brought out his new black-and-white soccer ball. Beans snatched it from him and booted it into the back of Mutto's head. Mutto squawked, and the two of them rumbled onto the sidewalk. Beans and Mutto rumbled several times every day. Each rumble lasted about twenty seconds, with both claiming victory.

The ball bounced down the street and into a neighbor's front yard. The front yards along Palmer's street were very small, about the size of a blanket. The grass was neatly trimmed, and almost every yard had a border of flowers. Most of the houses were gray.

Henry chased down the ball and kicked it back up the street. Henry always looked funny running, all arms and legs. He was by far the tallest of the group.

Beans said, "Which one is Fishface's house?"

Palmer did not want to say, but Beans was looking straight at him. "I'm not sure," he answered.

"Not sure?" Beans gave a smirk. "Guess I gotta start yelling then." He cupped his hands and yelled at the top of his lungs: "Fishface! Fishface! Fishface!"

Palmer pointed to the house directly across the street from his. "That one."

Beans stepped up to the house and shouted: "Fishface! Fishface!"

Palmer cringed.

No one came to the door, no window curtain stirred.

"Okay, Fishface, you asked for it!" Beans turned to Mutto and Henry. "Let's leave her a little present."

They searched the gutter.

"Sewer grate!" piped Mutto. The three of them raced to the nearest grate.

Fishface was Beans's name for Dorothy Gruzik. Beans and the guys hated Dorothy and harassed her whenever they got the chance. Palmer had never understood why, though now that he was one of them, maybe he would find out. Maybe now he could finally find a fish in her face.

Palmer's mother had been trying to push Dorothy and him together as friends for years. Palmer had never been much interested. For one thing, Dorothy was a girl. Plus she was in a lower grade and a whole year younger than he.

The guys returned from the sewer grate with something in a plastic bag.

"Just mud and sticks," said Beans glumly. He went to Dorothy Gruzik's house and dumped it on the top step. His face brightened. "Maybe they'll think it's poop."

He rang the bell, banged on the door, and everyone took off. It was the first time Palmer had ever run with the gang. He felt shivers of excitement. He screamed and beat them all to the corner.

4

They kicked the ball around for a while, then Beans said, "Let's go to the park." He booted the ball down the middle of the street.

"Why don't we play here," said Palmer, but the others were already dashing after the ball.

Let's go to the park.

Palmer hated the park. He never played there, never swung on the swings, never slid down the sliding board, never fed the ducks, never watched a softball game. Most especially, he never went near the soccer field. For in one month, four short weeks after his birthday, the soccer field would become, as it did every year, a place of horror.

He walked. Four blocks and he was at the park. He hoped they would be at the softball field but knew they would not. Nor were they at the baseball field or the basketball court or the tennis courts or the World War I cannon or the playground or the Boy Scout cabin or the picnic area.

He heard, then saw them at the soccer field, racing and yelping like puppies in a pasture. He stayed on the sidelines, walked along the chalked edges of the field.

"Come on, Snots!" they yelled and kicked the ball his way.

"Can't," he yelled, lying. "My leg hurts." To prove it, he threw the ball back. "I'll just stay here and watch."

He hoped they wouldn't be mad at him for not joining in. He loved to see them playing with his birthday present. Each thud of a foot said: *We're kicking your soccer ball. We like you. You're one of us.*

He wished it could stay like this forever.

But it changed. Beans backed up and pointed at Henry and yelled, "There's one!" Henry began flapping his arms and swooping in circles, being a bird. Beans and Mutto made their arms like shotguns and pulled the triggers: "Pow! Pow!" Henry veered, lurched, tilted, staggered. To Palmer, tall, gangly Henry did not look like a bird at all, but a giraffe with two howling hyenas snapping at its knees. It had long seemed a curious contradiction to Palmer, that among the three kids rollicking on the field, Henry was the tallest yet also the meekest. Palmer had the sense that he was seeing more than a game, that Henry was not just a member of the group, but also its prey.

After a minute or two of lopsided, long-legged careening, Henry flopped to the ground. "Wringer! Wringer!" shouted Beans. "Wringer! Wringer!" shouted Mutto. Four hands clamped around Henry's neck, shaking Henry's head like a rag doll, twisting it this way and that.

"Wringer! Wringer!"

Henry's legs flailing. Shrieking laughter.

"Wringer! Wringer!"

Palmer tried to hold the moment there, but it would not stay. It tunneled back through time and burst up onto this same field three years before, the first Saturday in August, when the grass was streaked with red and guns were booming and birds were falling. From the treetops, from the clouds they plunged to earth, thumped to the ground, sometimes with a bounce. And still some of them lived, flopping drunkenly across the grass until a wringer grabbed one by the neck and twisted and that was that.

Beans and Mutto were now at each other's throats, rolling, rumbling, rollicking across the grass, Henry woozy but up now, laughing with the others, then heading off with the others, the three of them yelping and kicking the ball up through the picnic area.

Palmer did not know why he stood there, alone at the edge of the field, the last place on earth he wanted to be. As the voices of his new friends died away, he was aware of the silence. He looked up. Nothing flew in the sky. Nothing called from the trees. For a moment a dragonfly hovered before his eyes like a tiny helicopter, then darted off. That was all. Silence and stillness.

He ran.

5

He caught up to them at the playground. They were diving headfirst down the sliding board—stacked, all three.

"C'mon, Snots, make it four," Beans called.

Palmer's mother had told him about sliding boards, way back when she started bringing him to the playground. Hold tight to the rail as you climb the ladder. No sliding down stacked. No sliding down headfirst. But this was a new time. He wasn't here with his mother, he was here with the guys. His guys.

"Snots, c'mon!"

He joined them on the ladder. As the stack arranged itself, he wound up on the bottom. He could not take a deep breath. He could feel the shape of his belt buckle in his stomach. He could smell the tinny slide. And down they went. And for the two-second trip, Palmer felt something more than the thrill of the plunge. He felt his friends above riding him, clutching him, depending on him. Had the slide been a thousand feet long, he would have carried them happily. And then they were spilling off the end like potatoes dumped from a sack.

Again and again they rode the slide, taking turns on the bottom. The first time Beans was on the bottom, he clamped the sides halfway down and stopped, sending the rest of them tumbling to the ground.

A lady called from the swings "Hey, you kids, no stacking."

Beans pinched his nose and honked, "Ehh, yer old man!" as they went flying down again. Mutto and Henry honked too. Finally Palmer did it, his back to the lady, pinching his nose, getting it out—"Ehh, yer old man!"—just before the giggles came, forgetting he hated the park.

Then Beans was pointing from the top step, shouting, "Look!" Everyone followed the pointing finger to a kid leaning against the monkey bars, a big kid, chewing on a beef stick.

Mutto gasped, "Farquar."

Farquar it was. Legendary wringer. The coolest, most feared kid in town.

Why was he staring at a bunch of nine-year-olds?

Beans called to Farquar, "Here he is." He was pointing at Palmer. "The birthday boy."

Suddenly Palmer understood. His birthday was no secret to Farquar. He was about to receive the ultimate honor, the ultimate test, The Treatment.

Farquar started walking. They followed.

Nobody gave The Treatment like Farquar. Palmer knew a kid who had his arm in a sling for a week after. Yet Farquar himself was maddeningly unpredictable. Some birthday boys he seemed to totally ignore, passing them on the street as he usually did, as if they were dog doo. On the other hand, he had been known to walk halfway across town, knock on a door and say sweetly to a surprised parent, "I hear there's a birthday boy in here."

Some kids turned into quivering zombies. They kept their birthdays as secret as possible. In school, if their teacher announced their birthday, they denied it, claiming it was a mistake. They refused to have parties. They stayed inside their house for a month so they would not bump into Farquar.

But there was another side to it. There was the honor. There was the respect you got from other kids, the kind of respect that comes to soldiers who survive great battles. There was the pride in yourself, in knowing you passed a test more dreaded and painful than any ten teachers together could give.

Farquar led them to the World War I cannon. The cannon was on a small grassy hill overlooking the park.

Farquar approached Palmer. With the end of one finger, he pushed the last segment of beef stick into his mouth. "Left or right?" he said.

Palmer had not known he would get a choice. "Left. No, right."

"Make up your mind."

"Left."

"Left it is," said Farquar.

Farquar rolled up Palmer's left shirtsleeve to the top of his shoulder, so that the entire arm was bare. Farquar studied the arm for a long time, pressing, feeling, like a doctor. Finally he said to Beans, "Put your finger right . . . here. Don't move till I say." Palmer felt Beans's fingertip on his arm, on a bony part about halfway between elbow and shoulder. Farquar spat on his own fingertip, rubbed the tip in dirt, and with the resulting mud—"Move"—made a mark on Palmer's arm where Beans's finger had been.

At this point, it was rumored, some kids wet their pants.

"Blindfold?" said Farquar.

Palmer looked over the peaceful scene: people playing, walking in the park, the trees, children's shouts. "No," he said, but nothing came out. His throat had turned to sand. He coughed, swallowed, tried again. "No."

"Okay," said Farquar, "don't move."

And don't look, thought Palmer. That's what he had always heard on the street: *If you ever get The Treatment, don't look.* By the time Farquar bunched up his fist and stuck out the knuckle of his middle finger, it was hard as a ball peen hammer and sharp as a spear. Bad enough you had to feel it. Don't make things worse by watching it coming.

Farquar took a position to Palmer's left side. He backed off a step, spread his legs, planted his feet firmly. He crouched, lowering himself. Palmer felt a gust of beef stick breath.

Beans and Mutto stood directly in front, grinning, as if watching someone about to get a hotfoot. Palmer wished he had asked for the blindfold. Henry was off to the side. Palmer took a quick look at him and wished he hadn't. Henry was not grinning. His eyes were wide as a hangman's noose.

Palmer turned back to find Beans's grin wider than ever. Beans had the most incredible teeth Palmer had ever seen. Beans swore he had not brushed them since the big ones came in. At one time or another Palmer had seen every color in the crayon box on Beans's teeth. Their major color was a dull yellowish-brown fringed with green.

Beans and Mutto shouted "One!" as the first rap hit, and Palmer understood instantly the genius of Farquar. He understood that Farquar somehow knew his body better than he himself did, that there was no need to rear back like a baseball pitcher and bring the whole fist. That when the perfect spot is found, the tip of a knuckle fired from a mere six inches away is enough—enough so that Palmer's whole body was sucked into a suddenly new sinkhole in his arm.

But Palmer kept his mouth shut. *Don't scream*, the street had always said. *If you do you'll get an extra.*

"Two!"

Tears sprang to Palmer's eyes, smearing the grins of Beans and Mutto. *Don't cry,* the street said, *or you'll get two extras.*

"Three!"

Palmer bit on his lip and screamed inside his head, bashed chairs and flung himself against the walls of his braincase: Stop! Stop! Stop! Stop!

"Four!"

He takes his time. You want it to be over fast but he goes real slow.

Henry had turned his back.

"Five!"

MOMMEEEEEEEEEEEEEEEEEEEEEEEEE!

"Six!"

"Seven!"

"Eight!"

"Nine!"

"What happened to your arm?"

Palmer's mother was lifting his shirtsleeve and asking him a question he did not want to answer.

"I said, what happened?"

"The Treatment," said his father, coming into the room. He mussed Palmer's hair. "Right, big guy?"

Palmer nodded. Even nodding seemed to hurt his arm. "Right."

His father inspected the spot. He whistled softly, he nodded gravely. "Nine hard ones, huh?"

"Right." Palmer stood a little taller. He felt as if his father had just pinned a medal on him.

But his mother's voice was strained. "What are you talking about? What treatment?"

His dad spoke for him. "It's been a tradition for years around here. On your birthday you get knuckled once for each year old you are. It happened to me plenty."

She sneered. "That doesn't mean it has to happen to him." She lifted his sleeve again. "Look at that. Look."

"It's a bruise," said his father calmly. "It goes away. He's okay. Right, big guy?"

Was he okay? His arm wasn't okay. It was killing him. But what about the rest of him? "Give him an extra!" Beans and Mutto had shrieked. "He's crying!" But Farquar had said no, it was just eye tears, everybody gets them. And he had carefully, daintily really, pulled Palmer's shirtsleeve down over the wound and said, "Happy birthday, kid," and walked off, and in that moment Palmer loved Farquar.

Was he okay?

"Sure," he said, and he gave a little chuckle just to prove it.

"Well," said his mother, aiming her voice somewhere beyond the room, "*I'm* not okay. He had those hoodlums here for his party."

"Beans?" said his father.

Palmer gladly answered. "Yeah, Beans was here. And Mutto and Henry."

His father wagged his head. "He's a pip, that Beans."

"Hoodlums," his mother went on. "And

they don't even like Palmer that much. They never pay any attention to him. They never play with him."

"They do now," Palmer protested. "They were just waiting till I was nine."

His mother ignored him. "He invites them, but little Dorothy Gruzik he doesn't even invite." She bore down on him. "Why not Dorothy?"

"She's a girl."

"She's your neighbor. She's one of your best friends."

Palmer laughed out loud. Sometimes his mother tried to make something come true simply by saying it. "She's not," he told her bluntly. "If she didn't live across the street I'd probably never see her."

"She invites you to her parties."

Palmer was fed up. Why did his mother have to go on the warpath just when everything was so great in his life? He blurted, "She has a fish face!"

His father laughed. His mother's eyes went wide, then she abruptly changed topics. "And the nickname," she said to his father, "you should hear the nickname they gave him for his ninth birthday, the hoodlums." She tapped Palmer on the shoulder. "Tell him."

"Snots," said Palmer. It was already beginning to feel like his.

"Snots," his dad echoed.

"Now what kind of name is that?" said his mother. "Where did that come from?"

Palmer shrugged. In truth, he had no idea. Beans gave out the names. His own obviously came from his appetite for cold baked beans out of a can, anytime, day or night. Mutto? A mystery. There was no dog in Mutto's life that Palmer knew of. And Henry, that sounded more like a real name than a nickname, but Palmer couldn't imagine Beans letting someone's real name stand, so Henry must be someone else too.

Seeing that no answer was coming from Palmer, his mother gave up and walked off muttering, "Doesn't have the good sense he was born with."

"Well, Snots," said his father, "sorry I didn't make it to the big party. Here's a present if you think you can stand another one." He reached into the dining room hutch and pulled out a gift-wrapped package.

Palmer tore off the paper to reveal an old, frayed shoe box. He gasped. He knew what was coming but still couldn't believe it. He lifted the lid. "Your soldiers!"

"Yours now," said his father.

They were twenty-seven toy soldiers. They were made of lead, which in many places showed through the olive-green paint. They were two inches tall, and they were very old. The helmets were shallow, like soup bowls. They had first been played with by Palmer's great-grandfather, then by his grandfather, then his father. Palmer had played with them many times, but only with his dad's permission. He had always thought of them as the most valuable things in the house. His dad kept them in the shoe box behind a suitcase in the back of a closet.

"That is," his father added, "if you promise to take care of them and pass them on to your own son some day."

Palmer could only nod in wonderment. "I can keep them in my room?"

"Sure can."

That night in his room Palmer debated where to hide the twenty-seven toy soldiers. He chose the high shelf of his closet, which he could not reach without standing on his chair. He had to carry the chair and reach up with his right hand. His left arm was useless. His fingertips tingled. At dinner he had let it just plop on the table and stay there. His mother kept glaring at it.

Sometimes his arm felt numb, as if he had been sleeping on it. But mostly it hurt. He found that if he kept his mind busy, he didn't notice the hurt so much. He read a book, watched TV, inspected his presents, thought about the day.

What a day!

New birthday. New friends. New feelings of excitement and pride and belonging. His mother was wrong about the guys never playing with him. He had had a lot to overcome, that was all. Being the youngest, the shortest. And his unusual first name, he took lots of teasing there. But that was all over now. He fell back on his bed, he grinned at the ceiling. Life was good.

While brushing his teeth that night, Palmer looked at his face in the mirror and suddenly began to cry. He cried so hard he could not finish brushing. He ran to his room, shocked and angry at this unexpected turn to his perfect day. Sobbing loudly, gasping for breath, he plunged into his bed and smothered his face in his pillow.

He was not aware of turning the ceiling light off and the night light on. He was not aware that he ever stopped crying. In his sleep a voice echoed down the long dark barrel of a cannon: *You have run out of birthdays.* In the morning he awoke suddenly to a flutter of wings.

7

The following weeks were like a parade to Palmer, with himself as grand marshal. He felt as if he were marching down the middle of a broad boulevard with crowds of people cheering from the sidewalks.

Calls of "Hey, Palmer!" and "Hey, Snots!" flew across the summer days. From blocks around kids came to see his arm. Little kids would gather around, four or five at a time. He would lift his sleeve, and they would gasp and go "Wow!" Some of them would reach out to touch. The squeamish ones would pull back their hands as if from a hot stove, and they would shudder and squeak.

Big kids did not touch. They simply looked and nodded in grim respect, remembering their own Treatment, and Palmer's heart would swell.

Within three days he could lift his left hand to his nose. At the end of a week he could reach above his head. He was almost sorry he was healing. He enjoyed showing off to little kids: "Look, I can't lift my arm any higher than this." He enjoyed the amazement in their eyes.

He wished the bruise would not go away. He wished he could make them feel the tingle in his fingertips. One day he darkened the diminishing bruise with a bit of purple crayon.

One person was missing during his imaginary parade down the boulevard: Dorothy Gruzik. And for some reason, this bothered Palmer.

Several times he saw her playing hopscotch in front of her house. Like Palmer, she was good at playing by herself. Of course, Palmer had buddies now, so he would never have to play alone again, not if he didn't want to. He wondered if girls grouped up like boys.

The first couple of times that Palmer walked past, Dorothy did not even look up from her hopscotch. This was very unusual. Dorothy had always said hi.

So next time Palmer said it: "Hi."

Dorothy just went on hopping one-footed, brown ponytail bobbing.

She's mad because I didn't invite her to my birthday party, thought Palmer. And that was understandable, but also beside the point. The point was getting her to look at the bruise, and the more she would not, the more Palmer wanted her to.

Finally he rolled his left sleeve up to the shoulder and plopped himself down on her front steps. She went on playing, tossing a green beanbag into the chalk-numbered squares, ignoring him.

At last he thought of a funny thing to say. "Who's winning?"

She said nothing. She tossed the beanbag to the farthest square and hopped on down and back. She tossed the bag out again, and just when it seemed she would never speak, she said, "Thanks for inviting me to your party."

It made no sense, but Palmer was thrilled to hear her voice. "It was all boys," he said.

"Good," she said with a disdainful sniff. Sometimes it amazed him that this girl, just out of third grade, could make him feel so little. She went on hopping.

"Did you hear my new name?" he said.

She did not answer, did not look up.

"It's Snots."

A short snorty chuckle burst from her nose, then she was stone-faced again.

He turned so that his left arm was fully facing her, so she couldn't miss it.

"I got The Treatment too." She went on hopping. "For three days I could only move my arm up to here." She did not even look. "Want to see my bruise?" Her eyes never left the green beanbag.

He stood. He smiled. "Want to touch it?"

It was as if he wasn't there.

So he ran off and found others to marvel at his bruise. He played with the guys, and when they came to taunt Dorothy, he did not feel as bad as he had before. They called her "Fishface!" and made fun of her name and kicked her beanbag off the hopscotch squares. Palmer stood back and gave a sly grin. *That'll teach you, Dorothy Gruzik.*

At the same time she befuddled him. Not once did she raise her eyes to her tormenters or say anything back. She did not run into her house. She did not cry. What kind of girl was this? She just kept playing hopscotch, as if no one else was there.

After a while Beans could not take any more fun, so they all ran off.

In the third week after The Treatment,

Palmer came to the end of his imaginary parade. His bruise had faded to a dim yellowish blot, and the crowds had gone home. But something was still there. Palmer knew what it was. It had been there all along, silent, hardly seen among the cheering crowd, a flash of black feather now and then, an orange eye, waiting.

As he kicked his checkered soccer ball along the streets, he could feel it lurking in shadowy doorways, behind shaded windows. He would not look. He felt it come out of the shadows, and the sunlight on the back of his neck turned to frost. It was behind him. He picked up his ball and ran.

But he could not run from time. It was the first week in August.

Family Fest had arrived.

Family Fest.

Such a nice name. And a nice time it was. A week of talent contests and softball games and races and Tilt-A-Whirl and bumper cars and music and barbecue and cotton candy.

And shooting pigeons.

If only Family Fest would stop on Friday, Palmer had often wished. But it did not. It began on Monday and ended on Saturday. And that Saturday, the first Saturday in August, one month after his birthday, was the worst day of the year.

During the night before, trucks could be heard rumbling through the streets, carrying wooden crates from the old railroad station to the soccer field. The crates held pigeons. Five thousand of them.

Except on that day, Palmer had never seen a pigeon in his town. Some, he heard, were trapped in the railroad yards of the great city a hundred miles to the east. The rest were bought, paid for. Why anyone would pay for a pigeon only to shoot it was just one of many questions about Pigeon Day that bewildered Palmer.

Palmer's first Pigeon Day had occurred when he was four. Certain moments, five years later, were still with him. The birds in the sky, then suddenly not in the sky, only feathers fluttering. The red fingers and lips of a man cheering, spewing specks of barbecued chicken. A man wearing a bright-pink baseball cap. The smell of gunsmoke.

And most of all the pigeon, the one pigeon that hurried across the grass lopsided—"loppysided," as Palmer would have said then—as if one leg had been kicked out from under it, hurrying, hobbling, wobbling in goofy loops, tilting like a sailboat blown over, a boy chasing after, running and reaching, the boy laughing, the people laughing, little Palmer thinking, *The boy wants it for a pet*. And then the pigeon was coming this way, flopping, righting itself, hobbling straight for the people, head bobbing, loppysiding on a curving course, and the people were shrieking and calling "Wringer! Wringer!" and the boy was chasing and sure enough the boy caught it, caught that hobblywobbling pigeon right in front of Palmer. And the pigeon's eye looked at Palmer and the pigeon's eye was orange and everyone clapped and Palmer clapped too and laughed and called out "Good!" and the boy closed his hands over the pigeon's neck and twisted his hands real quick—like *that*—and Palmer heard a tiny sound, like when a twig was stepped on, and when the boy took one hand away the pigeon's head hung down toward the green grass, so sadly dangled down, though the pigeon's eye was still round and orange.

Palmer had turned and looked up at his mother and said, "Why did he do that?" and his mother had said, "To put the pigeon out of its misery."

"Was the pigeon in misery?" Palmer asked his mother.

"Yes," she said.

"Why?" said Palmer.

His mother did not answer. She was looking at the sky.

"Because he was loppysided?"

She smiled thinly, she nodded. "Yes."

"The boy didn't want him for a pet, did he?"

His mother kept looking at the sky, kept not answering. Palmer began to notice a gray, sour smell in the air. Suddenly his mother grabbed his hand and pulled him away. As they squeezed through the crowd, the happy faces of the people and the cheers and laughter and the fingers red from barbecue sauce gave Palmer the feeling that he was leaving a party.

The boy, Palmer learned later, was called a wringer. It was his job to put the wounded pigeons out of their misery.

During the following year Palmer thought about that quite often. If the wounded pigeons were in misery, he wondered, why put them there in the first place by shooting them? Why not just let them all fly away?

Palmer's mother had no answer to these questions, so Palmer thought about it some more and concluded that all pigeons must be miserable, wounded or not, and that was why they must be shot. And perhaps the pigeons themselves knew this. Perhaps when the boxes were opened and they flew into the sky over the soccer field, they were not trying to fly away at all. They were simply giving the shooters a good target, they were saying, "Here we are, put us out of our misery."

How sad, to be a pigeon. And how nice of the people, that they would stop at nothing to help. They would shoot and wring—and, Palmer imagined, punch and hand grenade and bayonet if they had to—anything to end the poor birds' misery. And this, Palmer guessed, was why the people were so happy. Because every dangling, orange-eyed head was one less miserable creature to weigh heavy on their hearts. Heaven, Palmer thought with a smile, must be teeming with pigeons.

On the mantel of a fake fireplace in the den of Palmer's house stood a statue of a pigeon. It was golden. It was beautiful. Words were etched into a shiny panel below the statue. Palmer could not yet read, so he pretended that the words said: *In honor of all pigeons. This house loves you.*

But the questions did not stop. Killing the pigeons and putting them out of their misery stubbornly refused to mean the same thing. Palmer thought about misery, and it seemed to him that a shotgun was not the only way to end it. When Palmer was miserable, for example, his mother or father would hold him close and wipe his tears. When Palmer's mother or father put him out of his misery, they did not shoot him, they offered him a cookie. Why then on Pigeon Day did the people bring guns instead of cookies?

It was confusing.

"Was Daddy a wringer?" Palmer asked his mother one day.

After a minute she said, "Better ask your father."

So he asked his father. "Daddy, were you a wringer?"

His father looked at him and said, "Yep."

"Will I be a wringer too?"

His father gave a snappy nod and said, "Sure thing, big guy."

Sure thing. Palmer pronounced the words over and over in the days that followed. *Sure thing.*

Boys became wringers, he heard, when they became ten years old.

9

Palmer had attended his second Pigeon Day with Dorothy Gruzik and her family, as his mother had other things to do. It was Dorothy's first. She pointed to the mountain of boxes at the far end of the field. "What are they for?" she asked Palmer.

"That's where the pigeons are," he told her.

"What are they doing in there?" she said.

"They're waiting to get out," Palmer told her. He felt like an old pro, clueing in the new kid. "They go from the big boxes to those little white boxes there. Every little white box has five pigeons. Somebody pulls a string and a door opens and one pigeon flies out." His father had told him these things. "Guess how many pigeons there are."

Dorothy gave it some thought. "A hundred."

Palmer smiled smugly. "Five thousand."

Dorothy Gruzik's mouth fell open as her eyes rolled upward. She was imagining a skyful of pigeons. "Wow," she said. "Then what?"

"They shoot them."

For a long time Dorothy Gruzik did not move. It looked as if she were waiting for rain to fall into her mouth. When she finally turned her eyes back to Palmer, he wished he wasn't there.

"What?" she said.

"They shoot them," he repeated, and the words were dusty and bitter on his tongue. There seemed only one way to get rid of the bad taste, and that was to flush out his mouth with more and more words. "They go bam! bam! bam! They open up a box and the pigeon flies out and the gun goes bam! and the bird goes—" Palmer raised his hand high above his head and dived it down to the ground to show her; for sound effect, he tried out his newly learned whistle. "And then another one comes out—bam! Another one—bam!" After each bam! came a dive and a whistle. "And the wringers run out to get the pigeons, and if the pigeon isn't dead the wringer wrings its neck." He brought his curled fists together and snap-twisted them. "Like *that*." He made the sound of a twig breaking.

She was already running, tunneling through the crowd, bouncing off grown-ups' legs, her mother after her, "Excuse me . . . excuse me . . ."

Palmer bored through to the back side of the crowd. Dorothy was running past the picnic tables, her mother chasing.

Palmer called: "They put them out of their misery! That's all! That's all!"

He discovered that he was crying.

10

By the following year Palmer no longer cared to
watch. So he spent Pigeon Day at the playground with Dorothy Gruzik. Through the day
the squeak of the seesaw and the creak of the
swings joined the sound of the shotguns. At this
distance they sounded like balloons popping.

While they were on the swings, a boy he
knew as Arthur Dodds came by. Arthur had not
yet begun calling himself Beans. He was dashing
through the playground when he spotted
Palmer and Dorothy and skidded to a halt.

"Whattaya doing?" he demanded of the two
of them.

"We're swinging," said Dorothy. "What's it
look like?" Even then she wasn't afraid.

"They're shooting the pigeons," he said. His
feet were still pointed toward the soccer field;
his whole body was twitching. "Come on!"

"We're staying here," said Dorothy.

Palmer was glad that Dorothy answered, but
now Arthur Dodds was heading straight for

him. "What's your name?" he growled.

"Palmer."

"Your first name."

"That is my first name."

"What kind of a name is that?"

What could Palmer say? He shrugged.

Arthur Dodds came closer. At that time he still had his baby teeth, which were as colorful as his second teeth would become. "You coming?" he said.

Palmer did not know what to say. He looked at Dorothy. She was staring at him. Somehow her face gave him the answer. He shook his head no.

Arthur Dodds exploded. "Sissymissy! Girlbaby!" He gave the swing chain such a yank that Palmer was thrown like a bronco rider onto the ground. Arthur Dodds took off, braying, "I'm a wringer, I'm a wringer! I'm gonna get me a pigeon and wring 'im!"

And he did.

As Palmer later heard the story, Arthur Dodds made a real nuisance of himself that day. He kept darting onto the field to chase wounded pigeons, only to be chased away himself by the real wringers. Arthur Dodds, like

Palmer, was only five years old at the time.

Finally he got what he wanted. A shot bird, instead of falling onto the soccer field, made it to the picnic area before it came down. Arthur saw and lit out after it. He heard a woman screaming. The bird had fallen right into the pink-fringed stroller where her baby was sleeping.

By the time Arthur got there, the pigeon was on the ground and being chased around the picnic tables by half a dozen squealing toddlers. Arthur joined the chase. The bird flapped up onto a table. People screamed. Hot dogs flew. Arthur lunged across the table, knocking drinks, smashing pickled eggs, and snatched the pigeon by the legs in a bowl of chicken salad. According to the story, Arthur threw his arms into the air like a boxing champion and crowed, "Got me one!" Then, right before the gaping eyes of the picnickers, he wrung its neck.

Arthur Dodds wasn't finished. So proud was he of his dead pigeon that he took it home, wrapped it in newspaper and hid it under his bed. For almost a week he charged kids a quarter apiece for a look. Then his mother started to smell something, and pretty soon that was that.

Palmer smelled something too, something about his father when he would return from Pigeon Days. As often happened, Palmer would wind up in his father's lap. It was his favorite place in all the world, where he was safe from everything. But on those days he could smell the gray and sour odor of the gunsmoke. The closer he nuzzled into his father's shirt, the more he could smell it.

Then he began smelling the gray and sour odor even when his father wasn't there, even when Pigeon Day was over. It might happen in the morning as he sat in school, or at night as he lay in bed. It could even happen in his father's lap in the middle of winter, when the shotgun had been locked away for months.

The smell was sure to come on his birthday. It did not spoil his birthday, as it did not spoil his father's lap, but it changed those things so they did not feel quite as good as before.

Other things changed. Arthur Dodds became Beans, and Beans was joined by Billy Natola, who became Mutto, and by a new, very tall boy in town known only as Henry. Palmer wanted to join them, but they said he was too small and too young and that he had a funny first name and that he played with girls, little ones at that.

Which wasn't true. The older he got, the less he had to do with Dorothy Gruzik. When he went off to first grade, he left her behind on her front steps, clutching a doll. In second grade he said to the guys, "She's my neighbor, that's all. I can't help that, can I? And anyway, what do I want with a first grader?" But they weren't listening.

Palmer invited them to his eighth birthday, but no one came. So his mother stormed across the street and dragged Dorothy to the dining room table, and his mother and father and Dorothy sang "Happy Birthday" to him, and his mother had a big smile but her eyes were red.

That was the summer that Palmer's family went on a vacation trip. They stopped in the big city for a day. From the tourist information center they got a map and gave themselves a walking tour of historic places.

Pigeons were everywhere: sidewalks, ledges, steps. Palmer even saw one crossing a street with a crowd of people on a green light, just another pedestrian. They strutted boldly, those pigeons, going about their business, pecking here, pecking there. They did not seem in the least bit afraid or apologetic. They acted as if they belonged, as if this was their city as well as the people's.

And the people, they did not even seem to notice the pigeons. Palmer kept tugging at his parents: "Look, there's one! . . . Look at that one!" But the city people ignored them. No one had a shotgun.

Except for the wounded pigeon that was wrung in front of him when he was four, this was Palmer's first close look at the birds. He had heard that pigeons were dirty, filthy, nothing more than rats with wings. He looked and looked, but all he saw were plump, pretty birds with shiny coats. He was especially fascinated by how they moved. They did not hop, like sparrows or robins, but they *walked*, one pink foot in front of the other, just like people. With each step the head gave a nod, as if to say, *Yes, I will. I agree. You're right.* As Palmer saw it, the pigeon was a most agreeable bird.

They were passing through a park with many trees and benches when Palmer saw something that stopped him in his tracks. A man sitting on a bench was smothered in pigeons. They were on his shoulders, his head, his lap, snapping up seeds that the man appeared to have poured over himself. The pigeons were cooing and the man was giggling—or was the man cooing and the pigeons giggling? It was hard to tell.

Back home, it occurred to Palmer that since he now could read quite well, he should have another look at the inscription on the golden pigeon statue in the den. It said:

SHARPSHOOTER AWARD
PIGEON DAY
1989

There, standing before the golden pigeon, the odor of gunsmoke came to him, and he understood that his father was a shooter.

It was about then that Palmer began to feel a certain tilt to his life. Time became a sliding board, at the bottom of which awaited his tenth birthday.

Beans kept asking, "You gonna be a wringer?"

Every time, Palmer would look straight into that crayon box of teeth and say, "Sure thing." And every time he said it he could feel his heart thump. For among all the changes in his life, one thing stayed the same. It was something he had known since his second Pigeon Day, when he sat with Dorothy Gruzik on the swings: He did not want to be a wringer.

Cotton candy days, Ferris wheel nights. Family Fest was almost better than Christmas—and longer. What had been the American Legion baseball field last week was this week a wonderland. Ten times over Palmer explored every ride, every food stand, every amusement booth. He loved the boiling fat's crackling hiss that cooked his fries and funnel cakes. He loved the yelp and splash when a ball hit the mark at the Dunk-A-Kid booth, the pop of darted balloons, the St. Bernard-size grand prizes, Tilt-A-Whirl's woozy flight, neon lights like bottled fireworks, House of Horrors and Pretzel Man and chocolate bananas on a stick.

But in this year of Palmer's life not even Family Fest was pure and easy fun. Despite the gleeful shouting and merry-go-round music, he could not forget the soccer field at far end of the park: silent, waiting. At times the Ferris wheel seemed to be winching minutes, hauling him ever closer to Saturday and the boom and smell of gunsmoke.

He tried to avoid the guys, but it wasn't as easy as before. After The Treatment they had been showing him a newfound respect, and often they came looking for him. He began leaving his house by the back door. He kept his eyes peeled at the Fest.

Dorothy showed him no respect at all. He could have had a hundred Treatments and it would not have impressed her. And yet Palmer forgave her. He reminded himself that she was young and a girl and did not understand life beyond her hopscotch squares. Also, there was the memory of his second Pigeon Day shared with Dorothy. As the week raced toward Saturday, he began began to feel closer to her. But when he saw Dorothy's face flashing in the neon lights and called her name, she only stuck up her nose and turned away.

He rode the rides. His parents gave him money each day to spend. When that ran out, he used his own savings. He wobbled and swirled and tilted and whirled and plunged and soared. The closer he came to Saturday the more he rode.

The gang, whenever he bumped into them,

kept saying, "See ya Saturday, Snots. Six o'clock." They were supposed to meet at the World War I cannon. The shooting would begin at seven and continue all day.

When he was younger this was a matter of wonderment to Palmer. It became the means by which he could grasp the first really big number in his life: five thousand. For a long time five thousand meant the number of pigeons you could shoot in one day, one by one. As he grew a little older he discovered machine guns and tanks and bazookas and, of course, bombs.

"Why don't you just blow them up and put them out of their misery all at once?" he asked his father one day.

That was when his father explained how it all worked. He explained that there was more to it than putting the pigeons out of their misery. He said that only people who paid money were allowed to shoot the pigeons, and that the money was used to make the park better. "So you see," he said, "you can thank a pigeon for the swings at the playground."

And for a time thereafter, Palmer did just that. Whenever he swung on a swing, he thanked a pigeon.

Palmer knew that Beans and the guys intended to stay all day, from the first boom until the last gray feather floated to earth. When he went to bed Friday night he had decided what he would do: He would not show up at the cannon. If they came checking, he would be in bed, pretending to be sick. He would tell them that he had really wanted to go, but his mother wouldn't let him.

He felt good. The problem was solved. He went to sleep with a smile.

12

In his dream the pigeons came to town, not five thousand but millions. In their beaks they pinched the edges of the town, plucked it up and flew away with it, as if it were a Christmas tree display on a tablecloth. The only sound was the flutter of wings. Palmer wondered where they were going. They seemed to be leaving the earth behind. Ahead, all around, was nothing but space and the blackest of nights. On and on they flew.

Then he felt a spot of warmth on his face. A puff of light broke the blackness. He began to worry. Were they heading for the sun? Were they going to dump him and the whole town into that fiery ball? The light grew brighter. A pigeon was pecking him on the rump, pecking him and giggling. He squirmed to get away. He tried to scream, but instead of his own voice he heard another's saying, "Pinch him harder. Did ya get bare skin?"

He opened his eyes. The light was blinding,

then went away. It was totally dark. The night-light was off, and he was not alone in bed. *Somebody was in bed with him!* He started to make a sound, but his mouth was clamped by a hand. Somebody laughed out loud, somebody growled, "Shut up! They'll hear!" He smelled baked beans. The light reappeared. It was a little penlight. It shone on two faces. One of them said, "Shut up now, Snots, okay? It's just us, Beans and Mutto. Okay?"

Palmer nodded, and the hand left his mouth. He sat up. "What are you doing here? How'd you get in?" A glance at his window answered the question. The screen was up. His window was above the roof of the back porch. It could be done.

Next thing he knew he was yanked out of bed and onto his feet. "Come on," whispered Beans, "we got somewhere to go."

It did not occur to Palmer not to go along. Once the shock wore off, he realized what an honor had been granted him. Imagine: A month ago these guys ignored him except to tease him; now they snuck into his house and climbed into bed with him. Palmer LaRue. Amazing!

He turned on his nightlight and dressed, and out the window they went. From the roof edge they slid down a plank that Beans and Mutto had borrowed from a building site.

"Let's go!" barked Beans.

"Where?" said Palmer, but Beans was taking off.

They were a whisper through the nighttime town. By Beans's orders, they kept to the alleyways. They trotted in file: first Beans, then Mutto, then Palmer. The only sound was their sneakers patting the ground.

Never before, not even on New Year's Eve, had Palmer been up so late. Not to mention outside. Not to mention outside without a parent. It was not like Palmer to do this. He had always been an obedient kid. Lay down a rule, and Palmer followed it. He cringed at what his parents would say if they found out.

But the thrill of it, the honor of it swept all other feelings away. Jogging through the dark and sleeping alleyways, skirting pools of streetlight, he imagined he was a toy lead soldier come to life, following Sergeant Beans and Private Mutto on a mission behind enemy lines. He loved these guys. He would follow them anywhere. He wondered what other adventures awaited him in the days and years ahead.

They trotted through the park and past the National Guard Armory. They turned a corner, and they were at the old boarded-up railroad station. Palmer smelled something, like animals, and heard small, soft sounds. In the moonlight he saw a second building as tall as the station and nearly as long. He did not remember this second building. He began to hear that the sounds were voices, and he saw that the second building was not a building at all. It was a mountain of crates . . . and soft sleepy cooings. . . .

It was five thousand pigeons.

He stopped.

Beans and Mutto trotted on. They cheered and yipped and did a nutty dance before the stacked crates. Their mooncast shadows snagged on potholes in the old parking lot and pulled like black taffy. They made their arms like rifles and barked, "Bang! Bang!" and a squabbling uproar filled the night.

"Come on, Snots!" they called.

They picked up sticks and racketed along the slats. They played the crates like drums.

"Snots!"

Palmer could not move. Ten thousand orange eyes burned holes in his heart.

He heard a wrenching screech: they were ripping open a crate. What were they up to?

"Grab 'im! Grab 'im!" Beans was shrieking.

Ten thousand orange eyes.

"Got 'im!"

Palmer called, "I gotta go back! I have to go to the bathroom!"

He ran. He did not use the alleys. He ran down the middle of the streets, the middle of the lights, chased every step by the uproar of the crates, ten thousand orange eyes trailing him into his house, into his bed, under his sheet, into his sleep.

In the morning, Saturday morning, awakening, he heard tiny popping sounds in the distance. He closed his window, pulled down the shade. He brought his TV closer and turned it on loud.

Blessedly, they did not come for him. Still, to be on the safe side, he told his mother he was ill and stayed in bed all day. She looked at him a little funny at first, then was especially nice the rest of the day, as if he really were sick. She did not try to make him open the window because it was July. She turned on the fan.

He watched TV. He read. He cut out Beetle Bailey comics for his collection. His mother played cards and Monopoly with him. He did not play with his soldiers.

Several times, when the light was deeply golden on the windowshade, he heard the doorbell downstairs and his mother going to answer. She did not say who was there. He did not ask.

When his mother came in to kiss him good night, she turned off the TV and opened the window. The night was silent.

Nipper

13

"It's a doozie."

These were his mother's words as she sat with him looking out the living-room window. His father called it a blizzard. Palmer called it rotten luck.

It could have snowed on Christmas, the day he got his new sled. But it didn't. Nor did it snow the next day, or the next, or any day for the rest of the year. Vacation days, no-homework days—days that could have been filled with whistling plunges down Valentine's Hill were filled instead with hateful frowning at a cloudless sky.

The new sled was a classic: polished wood, red runners, steering handles. It no more belonged on the living-room rug than a Mazerati belonged in a stable.

On New Year's Day Palmer's father said to him, "You know, I swear the weather plays games with people. Every time I decide not to take an umbrella, that's when it rains. Maybe snow's the same way. Maybe we can fool it. Why don't you try putting the sled away, like it's spring and sledding's over for the year."

Having no better idea, Palmer dragged his sled down to the basement. He added touches of his own. He took off his shirt, wiped his brow and said, "Whew, sure is hot out these days. I can't wait to go swimming."

He put the sled in the farthest, darkest corner. "Won't be needing this thing, that's for sure." He covered it with an old blanket. He stacked cardboard boxes on top of it. He saluted, "*Adios*, old pal," and walked away.

This was mid-afternoon. At dinnertime he looked outside. He could not see stars. By seven o'clock the first thin flakes were falling. He stood at the front door and cheered: "Snow!" And brought the sled back upstairs.

The next day was the last day of the holiday vacation. He expected it to be still and white and waiting for sleds. Instead he awoke to a blizzard thrashing his windowpane. He looked out. The world seemed to have come to any icy boil. He could not see to the end of the backyard. He ran downstairs. A car, molded in snow, was stranded sideways in the street. The howling wind flung itself at the house with a fury that frightened him.

Even his mother shuddered beside him as she repeated, "A real doozie."

"I might as well chop up my sled," Palmer grumped.

She draped an arm around him. "Well, look on the bright side. If it's too bad to go sledding today, it'll probably be too bad for the buses tomorrow morning. Bet you'll have a snow day."

She was right. January third was a day for snowplows and snowboots, snowballs and sleds. It seemed like every kid in town turned up on Valentine's Hill. All day long Palmer, Beans, Mutto, and Henry made a quadruple-decker sandwich as the new sled sailed and resailed down the slope.

That day as a crimson sun fell below the rooftops, one weary and happy kid dragged his sled back to port. Before going downstairs to dinner, Palmer took a moment to look out his bedroom window. He had never cared much for scenery, yet the scene outside touched something within him. The setting sun seemed to have ladled its syrupy light over the crusted snow, so that ordinary house parts and backyards in this fading moment seemed a spectacular raspberry dessert. When his eyes fell to the porch rooftop just outside his window, he saw the four-toed imprints of bird feet etched into the snow.

A good thing there was no homework over Christmas vacation, for Palmer could never have managed. He was sound asleep by eight o'clock. And stayed that way until he heard the tapping.

This was unusual. His mother never bothered to knock in the morning, but came right in. "Who's there?" he said, his eyes still closed, his voice barely working.

There was no answer.

His eyes opened. It was daylight. "Come in."

The door did not move.

Had he been dreaming?

There—again the tapping. It was not coming from the door. It was coming from the window.

The guys!

Palmer was suddenly, sharply awake. Why would the guys come now, in the morning, before school? He got out of bed, raised the windowshade—and froze. It wasn't Beans. It wasn't Mutto. It was a bird.

More to the point, it was a pigeon.

14

Or was it?

So often had Palmer dreamed of pigeons, that's what he thought it might be: a dream. He pulled down the shade.

He walked around his room. He kicked his hippo slippers across the floor. He picked up his little foam basketball and lobbed some hook shots into the net hanging from the back of his door. He returned to the window. He lifted the bottom of the shade an inch. He peeked. He saw a pair of small, pink, turkeylike legs rising to a gray, feathery plumpness. He lifted the shade fully.

It was no dream.

Palmer flapped his hand. "Shoo! Shoo!" he whispered.

The bird pecked at the windowpane.

Just what Palmer needed, to be seen in the company of a pigeon. Beans would wring both their necks.

"Go! Go!"

The bird tapped, as if replying in pigeon code.

Palmer rammed down the shade.

What a stupid pigeon! A million towns to choose from all over the country, and this bird-brain picks the one that shoots five thousand of them every year. And of all the houses in town!

The door opened. His mother poked her head in, surprised. "You're up?"

"Just got up," he managed to say. "I heard you coming."

The door closed.

Palmer rushed through everything that morning. He couldn't wait to get out of the house. He was ten minutes early at the corner where he met the guys every school day.

They were two blocks away when they saw him. They waved crazily and yelled, "Snots! Snots!" and came running. They knocked each other into snowbanks in their attempts to reach him first. Palmer's eyes watered, he gave out a giggle, he felt so good.

The walk to school became one long snow-ball fight. Along the way Beans noticed Dorothy Gruzik walking behind them. "Enemy ambush!" he cried out. "Counterattack!"

The four of them fired volleys at her. She hunched and turned as snowballs exploded on the back of her red coat. Palmer could not remember seeing the coat before. Must have gotten it for Christmas, he thought, as he packed and fired, packed and fired.

"Battleship barrage!" shrieked Beans.

Palmer fired without restraint. Since summer he had hardly spoken to her. He had found out there just wasn't room in his life for both Dorothy and the guys. Like peanut butter and pickles, they didn't mix. It seemed like everything the guys liked, everything they stood for, she did not. Thanks to the guys, he finally saw her for the pooper she was. She never laughed, never had any fun. Even now, look at her—just crouching there, not a peep, no screaming, no crying, no running away like any normal girl. Always had to act so big. And three weeks ago, for the first time ever, she had not invited him to her birthday party.

The school bell was ringing.

"Let's go!" shouted Beans.

Giving it a little extra, Palmer fired a final

cannonball. It splattered white against the red coat, and he ran inside with the guys.

All day long he had a hard time concentrating. He kept thinking of the pigeon. Where did it come from? How did it get here? Did the blizzard blow it in? Where was it going now?

Anywhere but my house, thought Palmer.

After school he forgot about the bird in a flurry of snowballs and the crackle of sled runners on Valentine's Hill. He plunged and snowballed and tumbled and laughed until the sky in the west turned fiery orange. He made it home just in time for dinner. He did his homework. He played with his toy soldiers.

The sky outside his window was pitch-black. He did not want to look, but he had to. He got his father's flashlight. Slowly he raised the shade. He could see nothing but the reflection of his own room off the windowpane. He raised the window. Light spilled from his room onto the snow-capped porch roof. He saw pigeon tracks, but no pigeon.

He leaned out the window. He turned on the flashlight and swept it across the roof, back and forth, corner to corner. He saw nothing but silent snow.

He closed the window, lowered the shade, turned off the flashlight. He sat on the edge of his bed. He took a deep breath. He felt better.

15

Tapping.

Again, next morning.

Oh no.

He reached out from the groggies, lifted the hem of the shade two inches. There it was, the world's dumbest bird, dipping its dumb head down so its orange button eye could stare back at him.

Palmer knelt at the window. He talked to the orange eye. "Don't you want to live, you dumb stupid cluck? Go look at the soccer field. This town kills pigeons. There's a guy named Beans. He's my friend, but he's not your friend. He hates you. If he ever sees you he'll wring your neck. And if you don't care about yourself, how about me? What do you think's going to happen to me if people think I have a pigeon?"

He raised the shade; the pigeon's head rose with it.

"Please—*please*—" he put his palms together prayerfully—"go back where you came from.

We don't want you here."

The bird tapped on the windowpane. Palmer shook his fist and yanked down the shade.

Later during breakfast, as he chewed a spoonful of FrankenPuffs, he suddenly saw the issue: food. The bird was hungry.

Fine. So he feeds the bird.

But what happens then? Does the bird eat and fly away to the next town? Or does it return to the back bedroom window where it got its last meal?

Palmer was afraid he knew the answer. He knew that food was a powerful persuader of animals. Even his mother had told him once about a stray cat: "Don't feed him, or he'll keep coming back." If he fed this pigeon, it would be like sending it an invitation to return, an invitation to disaster.

That's why Palmer was surprised to find himself carrying a handful of FrankenPuffs up the stairs. And opening his window. And tossing the Puffs onto the snow, now crusted and gleaming with sun melt.

Puffs disappeared into the bird's beak. Palmer could not stop watching. Like the pigeons he had seen in the city, this one was mostly gray, the color of eraser-smeared blackboard. But there was more. As the bird pecked at the Puffs, sunlight skipped off glossings of green and purple around its neck. Palmer counted: gray overall feathering (one), orange eyes trimmed in black (two, three), tan beak (four), pink legs and feet (five), green and purple neck (six, seven), white wingtips (eight). Eight! Who would have thought one miserable winged rat had so many colors?

At the door his mother's voice, alarmed: "Palmer! I thought you were gone. School starts in ten minutes."

He slammed down the shade, prayed she hadn't seen. He loaded what needed loading—coat, boots, books—and ran. The sidewalks were empty, the guys gone. School came much too soon. He did not want to stop running.

All day long he was twitchy, runnerish. All day long he kept asking himself. *Why did I do that?* But he knew why. He just did not want to say, not even to himself.

After school he ran.

The guys spotted him. "Hey, Snots! Where you going?"

"Home," he called. "My mom gave me a job."

By the time he reached his bedroom he was gasping. He threw up the shade. The FrankenPuffs were gone. So was the bird.

He scanned the empty blue sky. How should he feel? He thought of the pigeon flying over the snow-covered land, looking for another window at another bedroom, and he felt bad. He thought of the guys coming over and not finding him with a pigeon, and he felt good.

He opened the window and with his fist crushed the crusty footprinted snow in front of it. No one would know a bird had been there.

He lay on the bed. He no longer felt like running. He wondered if pigeons flew south in winter, like geese. He wondered how far away it was by now. He thought about somebody else feeding the pigeon, and he felt jealous.

Then he felt nervous, realizing he was thinking of it as *his* pigeon, and what a dangerous thought that could be around here.

He got up. He got down his soldiers but didn't feel like playing. He put them back. He shot some baskets. He turned on the TV. He watched, but he wasn't paying close attention.

There was *Sesame Street*, with the Cookie Monster spewing crumbs all over the place. Then *Gilligan's Island*. The snooty, fancy-talking man was trying to crack a coconut with his wife's high-heeled shoe. He kept hammering until Gilligan snatched away the coconut and cracked it open by bonking it against his own head. But the hammering went on, right into the commercial . . . right into the commercial. . . .

Palmer sprang to the window. There it was. "Pigeon!" he yelped aloud.

His first thought was to feed it, so it wouldn't go away. He made a gesture of patience with his hands. Through the window he called, "Just wait there. Hold on." He raced through his room. He was always leaving something lying around—potato chips, pretzels, half a cupcake. He darted into the closet, dived under the bed, yanked open drawers. Nothing. Not a scrap.

The bird was tapping. It was still daylight outside, but fading.

"Just a minute . . . one second," he called.

He'd have to go downstairs, get something from the kitchen. Which was fine, except what if the bird got tired of waiting? Maybe, flying around all day, it had found a friendlier window, one that didn't make it wait so long. Maybe the next time it went away it would not come back, ever.

Palmer did not think. He did not use one bit of the good sense he was born with. He simply walked across the room and opened the window.

16

The bird walked in.

Not hopped. Walked. Like a person, like those city pigeons he had seen. Head bobbing, all business, cool as you please, like it owned the joint.

Walked across the windowsill onto the back of Palmer's hand, strolled up his right arm, nipped Palmer's earlobe—"Ow!"—and hopped onto the top of Palmer's head. Palmer stood rock-still, afraid to move even his eyeballs. Pointy little toes were moving in his hair. It felt scratchy good.

The bird made a sound like a chuckle, like it had just heard a joke, and in a wingflap was gone. Palmer turned and found it walking across the floor. Seen from behind, the pigeon waddled. Hunger had not been its problem—it was pudgy.

The bird hopped onto Palmer's bed and took a walk around, with each step nodding approvingly, as if to say *So far so good. I think I'll like this place.* Its orange eye never blinked.

It flew to the bookcase, ambled across the booktops, pecked at pages. It checked out the TV but did not seem interested in the program of the moment, the five o'clock news. It stepped through the circular UHF antenna like a show dog through a hoop, and moved on to the top of the dresser, where its waddle tipped over Palmer's family picture, the candle he made at school and everything else that had been standing. From there it swooped down to Palmer's stack of comic books. The landing was a disaster. As soon as the bird's feet touched down, the flimsy cover of the top comic gave way, and the bird—with a startled *Oh!* Palmer imagined—tumbled beak over toes to the floor. It left a white, quarter-size glop where it landed and marched over to the wastebasket.

Palmer yowled with laughter—just as his mother came in, asking, "What's so funny?"

Palmer stiffened. He blurted, "Nothing. Something on TV."

The wastebasket was behind the door she had just opened. He willed her not to look.

She frowned. "Why is the window open? It's cold in here."

He jumped up and shut the window. "Time for dinner?" Before she could answer he snapped off the TV and the light, pulled the door shut and bounded downstairs announcing, "I'm starving! Let's eat!"

When Palmer returned to his room after dinner, he did not see the pigeon. The white glop on the floor had dried to powder. He kept looking, in the corners, under the bed. Finally he found the bird in the closet, on the high shelf. It was resting on its stomach on the shoe box that housed the toy soldiers. Its eyes were closed.

Palmer emptied his pocketful of Franken-Puffs onto his homework desk. He took off his sneakers so he would not make too much noise walking around. He turned out the overhead light and turned on the desk lamp. He cleaned up the white spot on the floor.

He did his homework. He watched some TV. He mounted some Beetle Bailey comics in his collection book. He ate his snack. He read two chapters of a book. He did everything he usually did on a school night, except he did it more quietly. And with a warm, giggly, I've-got-a-secret feeling. And with a peek into the closet every five minutes.

When his mother came in to say good night and to ask if he had brushed his teeth, he knew it was time to have a talk with her.

"Mom?"

"Yes?"

She was standing in the doorway, her hand on the knob.

"Do you think maybe when you come to my room from now on, like, you could knock?"

He had tried to say it casually, in his best no-big-deal voice, hoping she would receive it just as casually and reply with a shrug, "Sure, no problem."

Hah! When did his mother ever make it that easy? She stood staring at him from the doorway, her eyes blinking, her expression a total blank, like he had just spoken to her in a foreign language. Then a faint amusement overcame her face, and she said, "Okay." Casually. With a shrug.

Amazing.

She smiled and closed the door.

Too amazing. What if she wasn't as casual as she acted? What if she came around snooping? He had to give her a reason.

He opened the door. She was halfway down the stairs.

"You want to know the reason?"

She stopped, turned, looked up at him. "Okay."

"Well," he said, "it's like, you know, I'm getting older now—" He stared at her. How could he say this?

She said it for him. "And you're a boy and I'm a girl, and you're getting too big for girls to see you in your underwear, even if the girl is your mother. So you want a warning, so you'll have time to cover yourself up. Right?"

He nodded. "Yeah."

"Just one question."

"What?"

"Aren't you still a little young for that?"

"I'm mature for my age."

She nodded thoughtfully. "Oh. I see." She started down the stairs, stopped, turned back. "How about, besides knocking, if I blow a whistle when I'm on my way?" Her eyes were twinkling.

"Mom."

"Am I still allowed to *wash* your underwear?"

Palmer closed the door. In another second he'd be laughing.

Palmer went to bed that night with a grin on his face. For the first time in his life, he was not the only sleeper in his room. He did not turn on the nightlight.

17

A pinch on his earlobe woke him. He opened one eye to find an orange button staring back. The pigeon was on his pillow, sounding like someone gargling water. Again it nipped his earlobe.

"Ow!"

Palmer swiped, and the bird flew to the foot of the bed. "I'm awake, okay?" Palmer wondered if his old pair of earmuffs was still around.

A knock at the door. His mother!

"Palmer."

"Yeah?" He threw his blanket over the pigeon.

"Time to get up."

True to her word, she did not come in.

"Okay. I'm up."

She went away.

The blanket moved like a ghost over his bed. He pulled it back. With a gobble the pigeon flew off to the comic book stack. Like the day before, it skidded off the top comic and onto the floor. This bird, thought Palmer, is either dumb, clumsy or a comedian. Palmer dressed and went down for breakfast. This time he returned not only with FrankenPuffs but Grape Nuts as well. He spread the cereal on the snow outside his window. The pigeon did not have to be coaxed. It flew out the window and attacked the food.

Over the next week Palmer got better acquainted with the pigeon and adjusted his own life to take his new friend into account. From the library at school he borrowed a book about pigeons. Actually he sneaked it out. When it came to pigeons, he did not trust anyone in town, except maybe Dorothy Gruzik. It occurred to him that if he walked up to the front desk with a pigeon book in his hand, someone might see him (though certainly not Beans, who avoided the library like toothpaste). Or the librarian might look at him funny. Or she might act nice and then as soon as he left report him to the authorities. So he slipped the book into his bag and walked out as innocent-looking as possible. He had it back on the shelf in two days.

From the book he learned that pigeons go to sleep as soon as the sun goes down. This was called roosting. He learned that it was okay to feed his pigeon cereal, but that outside on its own it would probably eat some gravel. The gravel goes into the gizzard and grinds the food as it comes down, since the pigeon has no teeth in its mouth to chew with. He learned that a pigeon isn't very fussy about what it eats, because its tongue has only thirty-seven taste buds.

He learned that a pigeon's heart is about the size of an acorn. And that a pigeon's heart, as measured against the size of its body, is one of the largest hearts in creation.

Palmer learned that in the wild pigeons used to live in the nooks and crannies of high rocky cliffs. When they came to this country, they headed for the things that looked like high rocky cliffs to them, which happened to be tall buildings and skyscrapers. And that's why pigeons live mostly in big cities.

He read about the passenger pigeon. Flocks of them numbered in the millions. So many were there that when they flew, they would block out the sun and people below would have to light torches. And then people began to shoot them. Even dynamite them. And by 1914 the last passenger pigeon was dead.

There's something about pigeons, thought Palmer, that makes people want to shoot them. Whatever that thing was, he could not find it in the book.

But he found much else. The book was eighty-nine pages long, and this surprised Palmer. He never would have guessed that there were eighty-nine pages' worth of things to say about pigeons.

But then, come to think of it, he himself could have written many pages about his own pigeon. (And no question now—it was *his*.) He could write about the pigeon tapping on the window every afternoon until he let it in. The pigeon strutting across the sill and onto his bed, then flying from spot to spot in the room, perching for a moment at every stop, as if to say, *Just making sure everything's as I left it*. The pigeon banana-peeling off the comic book stack in a clownish flop. Palmer finding his pigeon roosting in the closet every night after dinner.

And the sounds. So many, so different. There were tootles and grumbles and rumbles and sighs and gobbles and giggles and even a woof. His new roommate was a one-bird band!

He thought about a name. He thought

about how the pigeon nipped his ear each morning. In fact, it was always nipping at something: the Nerf ball, the gray soldiers, book covers. So there it was: *Nipper*. And simply because Nipper sounded like a boy's name, "it" became "he."

Before long a routine had developed:

Wake up. (The "alarm clock" being nips on the earlobe.)

Pretend to be groggy when Mom knocks with official wake-up call.

Let Nipper out. Leave food on porch roof. (He had bought a box of Honey Crunchers, which he kept in his closet. He had studied cereal boxes and found out that Honey Crunchers contained a lot of fat; and fat helps keep a pigeon warm in winter, so said the book.)

Clean room. Leave no evidence of roommate.

Go to school (or, on weekends, out to play). Act normal. Return home. Let Nipper in.

Nipper walks up arm, stands on Palmer's head. Feels good. Nipper checks out room. Nipper skids off comic stack. Laugh. Play ball with Nipper. (Nipper would perch on the basket rim while Palmer tossed in Nerf ball shots. As

the ball went by, Nipper nipped at it. Sometimes he caught it before it went through the
net.)

Go to dinner. Return to find Nipper roosting.

Homework, read, TV. Go to closet, whisper
"Good night, Nipper." Go to bed.

The hardest part of the routine came each
day when he left the house: *Act normal.* How
was he supposed to act normal in a town that
murdered pigeons?

18

Act normal.

In his room, in the streets, at school, seven days a week he whispered to himself: "Act normal . . . act normal. . . ."

But how could he act normal knowing there was a second pigeon right here in the house, a golden one that never took wing from the mantel in the den? Knowing that in this house, in this town, only the golden pigeon is allowed to roost. Knowing that he was holding inside himself such stupendous news.

Act normal.

He tried. Which is to say, he kept his mouth shut. He did not rap his fork on the dinner table and shout, "I have a pigeon!" Did not jump up in class and shout, "I have a *pigeon*!" He did not throw up his arms in the middle of the street and shout to all the world, "I HAVE A PIGEON!"

He did not.

But he did say to his mother one Saturday morning, "I think I'll change my own bedsheets from now on."

His mother was standing on a chair changing a lightbulb. As soon as Palmer said it, she wobbled on the chair, her eyes rolled. He was afraid she was going to topple. She looked down at him as if he were a stranger. "Would you repeat that?"

He repeated.

She finished changing the bulb. She got down and sat on the chair. "Is this another sign of your maturity?"

Palmer nodded. "Yep. And I don't even use the nightlight anymore."

She whistled. "What's next? Are you going to go out and get a job?"

"Just trying to help out," he said pleasantly. "And I'll empty my wastebasket too. And clean my room." He patted her on the head. "You'll never have to do it again." He kissed her on the cheek and walked off.

He could feel the stunned silence behind him. He was in shock himself. Was this him? He could not remember the last time he kissed his mother. He was not the mushy type. He was acting anything *but* normal. And he was beginning to learn how far he would go to protect his secret.

95

19

After dealing with his mother, Palmer turned his attention to the guys.

Certain scenarios gave him the sweats. It is afternoon, and the guys are in the backyard just as . . . Nipper swoops in to land on the porch roof. Or the guys sneak into his room at night, as they did before, and one of them . . . opens the closet door.

He toyed with the idea of coming right out and telling them they could never come to his room again. Tell them the room was crawling with cooties, or a ghost used to live there. But he knew that would never work. Telling Beans not to trespass would be as useless as telling Nipper not to peck.

Or he could tell them his mother said they were no longer welcome in his house (a lie). Because she didn't like them (the truth). But he didn't have the nerve to say it.

And so he tried simply to give them no reason to want to come to his house. One Saturday, for example, Beans decided they should all have lunch at Palmer's. They had done so a few times before, and Beans had always found something he loved in the refrigerator. Thinking fast, Palmer told them the refrigerator had broken, roaches had infested the kitchen, and they had nothing in the house but tuna fish and water. Beans believed him.

Another time, they had been playing outside in the snow and Beans decided he was too cold. "Let's go to Palmer's," he said. "We don't have heat," Palmer said. "Our heater broke." Beans said he didn't care; the house had walls and a door, didn't it? So that's where they headed.

Palmer could not think of anything until they were at his front steps, when suddenly he pointed across the street and yelled, "Let's bomb Fishface's!" By the time they finished snow-balling Dorothy Gruzik's house, it was nearly white, and Beans had forgotten that he was cold.

It became a habit, using Dorothy to divert attention from himself and his house. As soon as the guys would drift onto Palmer's block, he made his move:

"Let's bomb Fishface's house!"

"Let's bomb Fishface's car!"

"Let's bomb Fishface!"

When there was no snow on Dorothy Gruzik's sidewalk, they brought their own chalk and drew funny faces in her hopscotch squares. They ambushed her on the way home from school. They taunted her and ran rings around her as she walked. Sometimes they simply stood in front of her in the middle of the sidewalk, like human trees, forcing her to walk around them. Then they would run ahead and become new sidewalk trees, making her detour around them time after time, all the way home. Beans gave the game a name: treestumping.

One day Dorothy was not there. She was home sick. The snow had melted. There was nothing to bomb her house or car with. Every hopscotch square had been funnyfaced.

"I'm cold," said Beans, turning to Palmer. "Let's go to your house."

And Palmer, with no time to think, heard himself say, "Let's go to *your* house!"

20

Palmer had never been to Beans's house. He had been to Mutto's and to Henry's, but never to Beans's. He had come to imagine that Beans lived alone. Beans never mentioned parents, brothers, sisters or any other aspect of family life. Palmer further imagined that Beans lived by himself in a lean-to, or even better, a cave, a hole, down by the creek.

So he was surprised when Beans said okay to his suggestion. And even more surprised, ten minutes later, to discover that Beans did not live in a lean-to or a hole, after all, but in a house. And from the looks of it, a fine house, with a front porch and a shiny brass doorknob. Mutto rang the doorbell—which he did whenever he approached a house, even his own—and inside could be heard a two-note chime.

Beans took a key from his pocket and unlocked the door. He waved, "Come on in." Inside, Palmer looked about for signs of primitive living—mud, piles of rubbish—but saw nothing but clean furniture, carpets, pictures on the walls. A regular house.

Beans led them straight back to the kitchen. "Wait'll you see this." He dragged a chair in front of the refrigerator and stood on it. He opened the freezer compartment and began pulling out frozen dinners and plastic containers. Reaching in to the very back of the freezer, he pulled out a frozen dinner, jumped down from the chair and put the dinner on the kitchen table. The lid said spaghetti and meatballs.

"Yummy," said Henry.

"I hate spaghetti," said Mutto.

"You'll like this," said Beans.

The box was bigger than the others, a so-called "He-Man" size. And it had already been opened. Palmer could tell because the lid was held on by Scotch tape. Beans peeled away the tape. He seemed especially slow and careful about it. He looked up and grinned at each of them. He lifted the lid. It was not spaghetti and meatballs.

All three visitors recoiled. Henry went, "Eewww!"

Mutto was first to recover. He leaned in.

"What is it?"

Without warning Beans snatched the contents of the box and bopped Mutto on the head. "A muskrat!"

He threw it on the table. It clattered like a piece of wood. It was flat and stiff and mostly black, and Palmer never in a million years would have guessed it had once been a muskrat. Tree bark, he would have guessed, or sewer-grate flotsam. Now, staring down at it with the rest of them, he noticed clotted ridges that might once have been fur, and frost-fastened along one edge, a naked tail.

"Where'd you get it?" said Henry.

"Panther brought it," said Beans.

Palmer boggled. "You have a panther?"

Mutto and Henry laughed. "It's a cat," said Mutto.

Beans shoved him. "It's a panther!" He bopped Mutto again with the muskrat carcass, chased him once around the table and out of the kitchen.

While howls and thumps rang throughout the house, tall Henry leaned in close to Palmer and softly uttered, "Panther's a cat. It's the meanest cat in town. You can't pet it. It's always catching birds and mice. It bites their head off and brings the body to the front steps and leaves it there, like a present. Beans says Panther even killed a deer once." He searched Palmer's face. "You believe it?"

Unsure, Palmer stared back—and the hurricane swirled into the kitchen, Mutto screaming and laughing around the table, Beans waving the muskrat like a tomahawk.

Suddenly Beans stopped. He dropped the carcass on the table. He brought his hands up to the sides of his face, like paws; he crooked his fingers, like claws. He drew back his lip to show his teeth of many colors. He snarled, "Panther prowls the jungle. Panther stalks his prey. He waits, he creeps—" Beans crept across the kitchen on tiptoe. "He *pounces*! He *bites* the neck!" Beans pounced on Mutto's back. Mutto wobbled howling out the back door with half an inch of neck skin clamped between Beans's Technicolor teeth.

Outside Palmer met Panther for the first time. The cat was ambling into the backyard from the weed field beyond. Beans yelled "Panther!" The cat meowed, showing its daggery teeth. It was a yellow cat, ordinary-looking, no bigger than a usual cat. But ⎡

that no one, not even Beans, be   *the*

it as it ambled past the four of t

peared around the front of the h

Beans, hoisting the muskra

flag, blared, "Back to Fishface's!" and led them

out to the sidewalk. They were crossing the

street when Beans abruptly stopped. "Detail,

halt." He rapped his knuckles against the car-

cass, he shook his head disappointedly. "We

gotta go back."

Back to the house. In the kitchen Beans

placed the carcass in the microwave. He set it

for one minute, full power. At the end of the

minute, he tested it with his finger. He sniffed

it. He gave it another minute. By the third

minute Beans was the only one left in the

kitchen. The others were outside sucking fresh

air and trying to expel from their nose buds the

odor of warm, dead muskrat.

Beans finally came out carrying a super-

market bag. On the way to Dorothy Gruzik's,

Beans walked half a block ahead of the rest.

When he reached Dorothy's, he sprang into

action while the others hid behind a car several

houses away. Palmer could see Beans reach into

bag. When his hand came out it was holding the carcass by the tail. Again he reached into the bag, this time coming out with a hammer. He then nailed the tail to the Gruziks' front door, punched the doorbell and took off. He dived behind the car just as the door was opening. A lady—Mrs. Gruzik—appeared.

None of them saw what happened next, but there was really no need to see. The scream came as they huddled against the tires of the car. Palmer had thought he knew screams. He had heard plenty of them in the movies and on TV and at sporting events. But what he heard now was something else—it was real—and it sent icy buckshot through his body.

They heard the door close. When they looked up, the carcass was gone, and Beans and Mutto were on their backs, flinging arms and legs into the air and howling with boundless delight. It was during this celebration that Mutto, looking straight up into the gray January sky, said in a voice both dreamy and weary from laughter, "Hey, ain't that a pigeon?"

21

Beans jumped to his feet, looked up. "Where?"

Mutto pointed. "There." He stood. "It's gone."

"Which way?" said Beans.

Mutto pointed again. "That way."

Beans took off.

They caught up to him in an alley half a mile away. He was on his hands and knees, heaving clouds of vapor. "Got away," he gasped. He got to his feet but stayed in a squat, like a baseball catcher. His eyes scanned the sky. Then turned to Palmer. "The pigeon was flying over your house."

Everyone was looking at him.

"I never saw any pigeon around my house." Palmer forced out a chuckle. "I don't think Mutto knows what he's talking about. It probably wasn't even a pigeon. It was probably just a crow."

Mutto stomped. "It was a pigeon!"

Palmer shrugged. "Even if it was, so what? It

was probably flying south or something. What pigeon would ever want to stop off in this town?" He laughed.

"A *stupid* pigeon, that's who!" yapped Beans. They all laughed.

Palmer shouted, "I'm treating at the deli!" and trotted up the alley. He made sure to lead them well clear of his backyard.

Later, closing the door to his room behind him, Palmer broke down and sobbed. It had been a tense, uncomfortable day. The muskrat carcass. Mrs. Gruzik's scream. The pigeon sighting. He heard tapping. He opened the window, and before Nipper could step in he reached out and grabbed him in both hands and pulled him in. The bird squirmed a little but did not struggle to get free. Palmer ran his wet cheek along the silky feathers. He held him up.

"You *are* a stupid pigeon. Don't you know nobody around here likes you? Why didn't you pick another place to land?"

When Palmer set the bird down, it flew to the basketball rim and perched there, ruffing its handled feathers and holding its head high, prim as you please, as if to say, "Because I like it here."

From that day on Palmer became even more attached to his pigeon. Sometimes after school he would sneak out with the crowd, past the guys, and run home a different way to get there before Nipper. Once, he and Nipper arrived at the same time, and Palmer, dashing up his back-yard, suddenly felt familiar feet upon his head.

He wondered where Nipper went during the day. Did he fly around town, oblivious to the danger? Did he go to the park? Steer clear of the soccer field? Did he fly to other towns? For Nipper's sake, Palmer knew what he should wish. He should wish that Nipper would find another boy in another town, a town that would not run screaming after him, a town that would not hate him, would not shoot him.

But Palmer could not bring himself to make that wish.

Sometimes, when he let Nipper out in the morning, he would watch the bird eat breakfast out on the porch roof. When finished, Nipper would walk to the front edge of the roof, step onto the upturned lip of the rain spout, and with a chuckle take off. But he would not fly straight away. He would soar up and then circle the house once, sometimes twice. The library book had said pigeons do this in order to fix in their mind's compass the place they must return to. Palmer preferred to think the bird was reluctant to leave. In any case, Nipper then flew off and was quickly out of sight.

He was never clumsy outside of Palmer's room.

Although in the days that followed, the guys talked and laughed about the muskrat carcass and Mrs. Gruzik's scream, they stayed away from Dorothy's house for a while. But not from Dorothy.

They continued to snowball, treestump and otherwise torment her on the way to and from school. Palmer kept expecting consequences. He thought maybe her parents would show up at his front door. Or the principal would announce that they were all suspended. Or Dorothy herself would blow her top. When something finally did happen, it was not what Palmer had expected.

22

Treestumping had become popular among other school kids. Other boys, noticing what fun Palmer LaRue and his friends were having, decided this was something they could play too. So they began picking out girls to treestump to and from school. Occasionally a treestump got swatted by a girl's book bag, but for the most part the girls also found it to be fun, and before long they were treestumping the boys. Dorothy Gruzik, of course, being the exception.

Beans began to notice. For a while it had been enough just to bother Dorothy Gruzik, enough to hear the laughter of himself and his pals. Now he wanted more. He wanted something from Dorothy. He wanted her to scream or laugh or cry or kick or sling a book bag. Or even scowl. A good scowl, that would do for starters. Anything but ignore them.

For that's what Dorothy did. Except to walk around them when they planted themselves in front of her, she in no way acknowledged their existence. She did not even look at them. One day after school, determined to change this, Beans ordered the guys to meet her right at the school door and to treestump her, if necessary, every step of the way to her own front door. They did. Not once did she look at them.

Nor did she make it harder for them. She could have taken shortcuts through people's yards. She could have gone into a store here, a friend's house there. But she did not.

Beans began to do more. Instead of just standing stiff and stumplike in front of her, he waggled his arms and legs. He rolled his eyes and wiggled his ears. He stretched his lips to show every one of his multicolored teeth. He grunted and bellowed and snorted and just plain screamed in her face. He scooped a plastic spoonful of baked beans from his can and dumped it onto her shoe.

The guys and the other kids howled with laughter. Palmer's stomach hurt, he laughed so hard. That Beans! He looked like a puppet on strings herkyjerking in front of Dorothy, his head wobbling, even his ankles. What a clown!

Dorothy never flinched, she never looked.

On a windy day Beans swatted her books

away, making papers fly, so she had to go chasing them. Another day he snatched away her floppy red hat and put it on his own head and did his goofy, flailing dance in front of her.

The sidewalks erupted in laughter. Even passing cars slowed down. Dorothy did not crack a smile. She did not step aside. She did not step back. She did nothing. She did not even leave the hat at home next day.

In the following days Beans zeroed in on the hat. He sent it flying across the street. He tossed it into a Dumpster. He hung it from a car's antenna. He tacked it to a telephone pole. He wiped a window with it. For Mutto, Henry and Palmer, who by now were strictly spectators, this was a daily after-school show.

Each morning the hat was a little grayer, a little less red, and just as firmly on Dorothy's head.

Mutto said in amazement, "I think she *likes* torture."

Beans smoldered.

The last thing Beans did was the simplest of all. It happened on a Friday afternoon. As usual, he intercepted Dorothy on the way home. But this time he not only stepped in front of her—

he closed in. He closed in until there was barely a paper's width of space between their noses. No monkeyshines this time, no funny faces. His jaw hard, his eyes burning, he stared unblinking into eyes a mere inch away and dared them not to see him. Dared her not to smell his baked-bean breath.

All movement, all laughter on the sidewalks stopped. The boy and the girl stood like that for what seemed like hours, so close that at a distance it seemed they might be kissing. And to those nearby, and finally to Beans himself, it became clear that even now, even this close, still—*still*—she would not look at him.

And then she did it.

She spoke.

But the person she spoke to was not Beans. It was Palmer LaRue. She took one step back from Beans and walked straight over to Palmer and stood squarely in front of him and said, "Why are you doing this to me?"

And just like that, the girl in the red coat and floppy hat was no longer a target. She was Dorothy, there were tears in her eyes, and she was saying to him, not to anyone else, but to him, to Palmer, "Why are you doing this to me?"

And he knew that through these last weeks she had been hurting after all, and that it had been himself, not Beans, who had hurt her the most.

She turned away then, not bothering to wipe her eyes, and walked home.

The next day Nipper failed to return. As usual, the first thing Palmer did after closing his door was to look to the window. Usually what he saw was Nipper's silhouette, a clear black cutout on the golden sunlit shade. This time there was only the shade like an empty movie screen.

Well, it had happened before. Sometimes Palmer was the first to get home. He shot baskets with his Nerf ball, glancing at the window after every shot, listening for taps on the pane. With every passing moment he became convinced something was wrong, this was not an ordinary delay. In a way more felt that thought, he sensed a connection between Nipper's absence and Dorothy's words, which had been haunting him without letup.

He raised the shade, raised the window, looked out. No Nipper. Not on the roof, not in the sky. And the sun was behind the houses. Nipper had never been this late before.

He shot baskets. He searched the sky. He watched the clock. Cooking smells drifted up to his room. Daylight faded. His mother called, "Palmer, dinner!" He pounded his fist on the windowsill, he kicked the bed. Tears came.

He told his parents he had to watch the news for a school project and got permission to take his dinner in his room. But he could not eat. He could not do anything but wait and watch and listen—and try to forget how useless waiting was. For he knew that no pigeon flies after sundown, and wherever Nipper was, he was there for the night.

And where could that be? Had he gotten lost? Found another pigeon? Another human friend? Was he roosting warmly in another closet in another town? Or on a road somewhere, crushed, nothing of him moving except a wing waving with every passing tire?

Had Panther the yellow cat got hold of him?

He pounded his fists on his thighs and squeaked in frustration. He wanted to do something, but what? What do you do when your pigeon does not come home? He went out to the backyard. He stood in the cold night and looked up and softly called, "Nipper . . . Nipper? . . ."

A world of stars and darkness gave no reply.

In the den he whispered to the golden bird, "Where is my pigeon?" The golden bird was silent.

He did not go to sleep that night. Instead, sleep sneaked up on him, and the next thing he knew he was dreaming of a tapping, a cruel dream of a pigeon tapping on the window. Only it wasn't a dream, for his room was filled with daylight pouring under the raised shade, and there was Nipper, pecking at the pane. When Palmer opened the window, Nipper, as usual, hopped onto his head—and bent down and gave his ear an especially ouchy nip, as if to say, "Who said you could wake up without me?" No Christmas morning was ever happier than that one.

It was Saturday, so the two could play as long as they wished. Palmer kept the bird in his room until noon. By that time Nipper was knocking on the window, clearly wanting to go out. Palmer hated to let him go, but he knew he must. As he opened the window and watched Nipper fly off, he knew something else: He could no longer bear this alone. It had to be shared.

Why are you doing this to me?

He dashed down the stairs, out the door and across the street, coatless, not feeling the cold. He knocked on her door. He pressed the doorbell. Inside he heard her footsteps, her voice calling, "I'll get it!"

The door opened. Warmth and light washed over him. She smiled. She was glad to see him. He did not wait another moment. He said, "I have a pigeon."

Featherfall

23

Beans's mother—Palmer had to fight the temptation to call her "Mrs. Beans"—was a perfectly normal-looking woman whose teeth were as white as the icing on her son's tenth birthday cake. Waving her arms like a conductor, she led them in a raucous "Happy Birthday" and dished out generous gobs of ice cream.

As soon as Beans tore open his presents—baseball from Palmer, pocketknife from Henry, Campbell's baked beans from Mutto—Mutto called out, "Treatment! Treatment!" and dragged Beans outside. The gang headed up the street to Farquar's house.

Mutto banged on the front door. "Farquar! Farquar!"

No one answered. They circled the entire house, Mutto rapping on every window and door he could reach. He threw out his arms. "Nobody home."

And then a strange thing happened.

Beans, instead of being relieved that his arm

was spared, said, "Let's find him," and trotted off after his own Treatment.

"You're crazy," said Henry, who, like any normal kid, hated The Treatment. Henry always had to be prodded to face Farquar. "Why do you want to go looking for it?"

"'Cause I ain't ten till I get The Treatment," said Beans.

In a sense, this was true. Among the four friends, there was the feeling that neither calendar nor cake made a birthday, not officially. For it to be official, your arm had to feel the sting of Farquar's knuckle. It was a dilemma: you wanted to be a year older, you did not want The Treatment, and you couldn't have one without the other. At the very least, it slowed you down. For once in your life, you were not in a hurry.

But Beans was in a hurry, trotting through town, checking out Farquar's usual haunts, knocking on the doors of his friends, calling out his name. Beans seemed anxious at first, then frantic, as if not finding Farquar would condemn him to being nine forever.

They finally found Farquar kicking a ball on the soccer field. As Beans, then Mutto and

Henry ran, Palmer lagged behind. The day could not have been more pleasant. The sky was blue, the air warm. The crack of baseball bats could be heard in the distance. Newborn leaf clusters on the surrounding trees had a look of pale green popcorn. Tufts of onion grass sprouted across the soccer field, releasing their sweet scent. But the scent that entered Palmer's nose was the sour smell of gunsmoke. The soles of his feet tingled as he walked upon the ground that halted the fall of thousands.

Beans's eyes were shining, his face excited as he accepted The Treatment. When Farquar finished, he noted Beans's face registered no pain. He frowned at his famous knuckle. He bent into Beans's face for a better look. "You okay?" he said.

Beans threw both arms into the air, as if one of them had not just been demolished. "I'm great!" he shouted. "I'm ten!" He backed off then, until he stood alone in the field. No bird sang in the trees, no wing flew overhead. Beans made a fist of both hands and held them out before him, end to end. The grin on his face tilted, his teeth appeared, a squitchy sound came from his throat, the two closed fists snapped in opposite directions. He crowed, "And I'm a wringer!"

Palmer shivered. His own birthday was three months away.

24

Palmer came home that day to find Dorothy shooting baskets in his room.

"I asked your mother if I could come in," she said, "so I could play basketball."

Palmer sniffed. "That's a lie. You're here for Nipper." He glanced at the window. The pigeon was due home any minute.

Dorothy laughed and bounced the weightless ball off Palmer's forehead. "Stop me," she growled, scooping up the ball, and suddenly she was leaping into him, over him, her knees in his chest, jamming the ball into the four-and-a-half-foot-high basket and shrieking, "In your nose, out your toes!"

She laughed and bounced the ball off his nose. When he got over the shock, Palmer joined her, the two of them flinging the ball at each other and cackling like a pair of chickens.

Palmer wasn't surprised to find Dorothy in his room. Since he had told her about Nipper, she had come over often. His mother, thrilled that Dorothy was back in his life, received her like a daughter.

As for the Beans Boys, as they sometimes called themselves, by spring they had tired of tormenting Dorothy and pretty much ignored her. Still, she did not come over when they were around. And whenever she saw Palmer with them at school, she acted as if she did not know him. Palmer sensed that she was doing this for his sake.

Dorothy sat on the edge of Palmer's homework desk.

"So, how was the big party, *Snots?*" she said with a sneer.

Palmer shrugged. "Okay."

"What gross stuff did you do, you and your best friends? Did you eat a dead muskrat, *Snots?*"

"Not really. And don't call me Snots."

"Why not? That's your name—*Snots*—isn't it, *Snots?*"

When Dorothy talked this way, Palmer could not always tell if she was serious. "It's just my gang name."

"I sure am sorry I'm not in the gang," Dorothy said. "Look at all the great stuff I'm missing. No neat name for me. No dead muskrats. No torturing people on the way home from school. No making mothers scream. No Treatment on my birthday." She rolled up her sleeve. She put on a pouty face. "Look at that, Snots, not one bruise. I want a black-and-blue arm. I want to have to do everything with one hand. I want some pain."

Palmer's middle knuckle rose from his fist. He came at her with a wicked grin. "Okay—"

Dorothy screamed and hopped from the desk. They reeled about the room, she screaming, he laughing, and it wasn't until they quieted down that they heard the tapping.

"Nipper!"

Nipper was let in, and as usual went straight to the top of Palmer's head. This brought a complaint from Dorothy. "He never stands on my head. I want him to stand on my head."

"Hold still," said Palmer. He leaned in toward Dorothy until their foreheads were touching. "Go ahead, Nipper, go to Dorothy." Nipper would not move from his perch.

Dorothy stomped her foot. "Phooey."

"Wait a minute," said Palmer excitedly. He transferred Nipper to the basket rim, left the room and returned a minute later. "Nipper has a thing about ears," he said. "Especially if there's something *in* your ear. One day I had an earache and I had one of these in my ear." He held up a small wad of cotton. "He kept pulling it out."

Dorothy took the cotton wad and pressed it into her left ear. "Yoo-hoo, Nipper," she called, "look what's in my ear." She stood in the middle of the room with her left ear to the rim. Without delay Nipper flew to her head, bent down and plucked out the wad. He flew back to the rim and let the wad fall through the net.

Palmer and Dorothy cheered: "Two!"

Palmer scooped up the foam ball, slam-dunked it and thrust his chin at Nipper. "In your face, bird."

Nipper nodded and pecked him on the nose. Dorothy cracked up.

They were laughing and playing ball when Palmer, letting fly a long shot from beyond the bed, said, "Do you like my father?"

Dorothy watched the ball bounce off the door. "What kind of question is that?"

"Do you?"

"Sure, why?"

"Do you think he's nice?"

"Yeah, don't you?"

Palmer thought for a moment. "Yeah, he is. I guess that's the problem."

Dorothy rolled her eyes. "You're talking goofy. What problem?"

"The golden bird."

Dorothy threw the ball at him. "Will you please make some sense."

Palmer looked across the room at Dorothy. She was back on his homework desk. Brown hair funneled into a ponytail by a plain rubber band. Pale-blue T-shirt. Jeans. Black-and-white sneakers swinging above the floor. Same old across-the-street Dorothy he had known all his life.

And yet, somehow, not the same old Dorothy. Though she looked the same as always, Palmer had been seeing something else in her lately. Whatever it was, it registered not in his eyes but in his feelings, and was most clearly known to him by its absence in the company of anyone but her. It made him feel floating.

The previous summer Palmer's mother had taken him to the outdoor Y pool for swimming lessons. The first lesson was floating. The instructor told him to just throw back his head, bring up his feet and allow himself to lie on his back on the water. This made no sense to Palmer. All of his life's experience told him that if he left his feet, he would fall, or in the case of water, sink.

"Relax," the instructor kept saying. "Trust the water. It will hold you up."

But Palmer could not trust the water. For many days he could not trust it. And then, with the instructor promising not to let him sink, he tried. With the instructor's hand on the small of his back, he tilted back, back until he felt water on his neck, on his ears. The instructor's hand pushed gently upward, Palmer's feet left the floor of the pool . . .

"Lie back . . . relax," said the instructor. "Pretend it's your bed. Trust it."

He lay back, he tried to trust. He could see nothing but the instructor's face and, beyond, the vast blue sky. And then the instructor's face was gone, his hand was gone, and his voice was saying, "You're floating."

Palmer got the same feeling with Dorothy. He knew that he could let go, and she would hold him up.

Tears filled his eyes. He let go. "I don't want to be a wringer. But everybody else is a wringer when they're ten, and I'm going to be ten in seventy-one days, and then I'm going to have to be a wringer too but I don't want to. So what kind of a kid am I? Everybody wants to kill pigeons but me. What's the matter with me?"

He said it all. He said things he had been thinking and feeling for years. He said things he didn't even know he had been thinking until he heard them come out of his mouth. He told her how he hated the golden bird, the trophy his father had won one year for shooting the most pigeons. He told her it confused him. How could one person be both a shooter of pigeons and a loving father?

He apologized for joining in on the treestumping and for calling her names. "You don't really look like a fish," he said.

"Oh thank you," she said.

He apologized for not inviting her to his last birthday party. He apologized for the muskrat carcass.

"My mother was shaking," she said.

He told her about Beans's party and the night they came for him in his bed and led him to the railroad station and the boxes of birds. He told her about the time Nipper flew overhead and was seen by the guys and how scary it was to be the only person in town with a pigeon and about his dreams at night. He told her that sometimes he wished he had not joined up with the guys after all, and he told her again and again that he did not, he really did not want to be a wringer.

Dorothy hopped down from the desk. She walked across the room and stood before Palmer and looked straight into his eyes. "Then don't," she said. She made it sound so simple.

Palmer snickered. He got up from the bed, kicked the ball around. "Yeah, don't. Easy for you to say, you're not a boy. You didn't grow up all your life scared to be ten."

"I have an idea," said Dorothy brightly. "Why don't you just skip ten and go right to eleven? Or tell everybody your birth certificate was wrong and you just found out you're really twenty-one."

Palmer stomped his foot, sending Nipper in a flutter from the basket rim. "It's not funny!"

Dorothy shrugged. "Well, you didn't like my serious answer—if you don't want to be a wringer, *don't* be a wringer." She sat on the bed.

Palmer shrieked, "I *can't* not be a wringer!" Nipper flew to the bedstead. "Everybody is a wringer. You *have* to be a wringer. That's how it always was. You don't know, you're a girl. What do you think"—he sneered into her face—"I can be the only boy in the history of the town who was ever not a wringer? And what makes you think"—he poked his finger at her—"what makes you think Beans would ever let me get away with it? They would drag me out of this bed and out to the park. They would wring *my* neck."

From her seat on the bed, Dorothy stared at the poking finger. She took hold of it and pulled it, drawing Palmer closer until his face was inches from hers. At that point she grabbed his earlobes and pulled him closer still. She smiled broadly. She kissed the end of his nose and laughed.

Palmer froze for a moment, stunned, then crumpled into laughter himself. They laughed and played games with Nipper for the rest of the afternoon.

25

For much of his life Palmer LaRue had felt he was standing at the edge of a black, bottomless hole. On the fifty-ninth day before his tenth birthday, he fell in.

Daffodils clustered like bugle bands in front yards as the Beans Boys left school behind on a sunny, cloudless day. It was a day in which everything seemed possible, the only problem being to make a choice. Beans wanted to head for the creek to hunt salamanders. Mutto craved a stone fight. Henry felt like baseball. And Palmer, he couldn't decide, or rather, he didn't want to decide. He simply wanted to enjoy: the bright spring day, the company of his friends. There was nothing he wanted to do—he simply wanted to be. But this was not something he could explain to himself, much less to the guys.

They came to the corner of Maple and Kane and stopped. A decision had to be made which way to go. Palmer was about to throw his vote to baseball when suddenly the sunlight was

briefly snipped, as if a page had been tu
front of a lightbulb. This was followed
by a flapping sound, the feel of a pair
toed feet in his hair, and the deep-throated tre-
ble of a familiar voice. Palmer's mind riffled
through a thousand answers to account for all
this, but only one made sense: Nipper had just
landed on his head.

Three mouths gaped open; six eyes, round
as tiny planets, stared. Suddenly Beans's face
became a red, shrieking mask: "PIGEON!"
Hands reached, wings flapped, the four-toed
feet were gone from his head.

Knowing at once how he must act, Palmer
looked up at the fleeing bird. "Hey, come here!"
he called, reaching up, running after it. "Hey,
bird, get down here!"

The others too were running, reaching,
shouting. They gave chase for a full block until
the gray flyer vanished over the rooftops.

As they slowed to a walk, Palmer began to
talk. "Man, did you see that? Do you believe it?
Where did that thing come from? I thought
I was gonna have a heart attack. You sure it
was a pigeon? What would a pigeon be doing
around here? Maybe it was a crow. It kinda

looked like a crow to me."

"It was a pigeon," said Beans. His voice was not friendly.

Palmer did not return Beans's stare. "Really?" He pretended to scan the skies. "If that thing ever comes near me again"—he made a chopping motion—"I'll whack it." He bent down and showed the top of his head to the others. He ruffled his hair. "Did it poop on my head?"

No one answered. He straightened up. He dared not look at them. They walked in silence. He felt their eyes. His heart was thumping.

"The bird is yours." Beans's voice, from behind. Palmer turned. They had stopped ten steps ago. It felt like ten miles.

Palmer spread his arms, he crouched as if to leap from a high place. *"What?"*

Mutto pointed. "It's *yours*, ain't it? That's why it landed on *your* head."

"And that one we saw fly over us that time on your street," said Beans.

"Yeah!" croaked Mutto.

Palmer laughed. "You're crazy! Why would I have a pigeon? I hate pigeons. I'm gonna be a wringer. I'm gonna wring their necks. I'm gonna whack 'em." An empty soda can was lying in the gutter. He stomped on it with all his might, stomped again and again, crushed it, flattened it. He picked it up and dashed it to the sidewalk and stomped on it some more. "Whack 'em! Whack 'em! I hate pigeons! I hate 'em all!" He looked up at the staring, glaring eyes. He clenched his fists, he screamed: "I'm gonna be the best wringer there ever was!"

26

An hour later in his room with Dorothy, Palmer was still jumpy. He paced back and forth, telling Dorothy what had happened. The more agitated he became, the faster he paced. Nipper observed from a booktop, swinging his head as if watching a Ping-Pong match. The bird had been waiting at the window, as usual, when Palmer returned home.

"Sit down," said Dorothy, who sat on the homework desk, "you're making me nervous."

"I can't help it," said Palmer. "I almost got killed out there."

"Palmer, they kill pigeons in this town, not people."

"That's what you think. You didn't see the way they we looking at me. And don't say"—he formed the words *kill pigeons* with his lips— "around him." He nodded toward Nipper, who had stopped and cocked his head, as if listening.

"Sorry," said Dorothy. "So what are you going to do?"

Palmer threw out his arms. "I don't *know!*" He spoke to Nipper. "You dumb stupid bird-brain. Why did you do that? What am I gonna do?" When he had come home and found Nipper at the window as usual, he was both happy and not happy. He half wished Nipper hadn't showed up, so he could be rid of the whole problem. For a moment he considered pulling down the shade, then hated himself for even thinking that and threw open the window.

He took two fistfuls of his own hair, squatted on the floor and screamed up at the pigeon. "What am I gonna *do?*"

Nipper's answer was a gargling noise.

"Teach him to shoot fowl shots. Get it? F-O-W-L?" Dorothy tittered at her own joke. Palmer wasn't amused.

Dorothy had Palmer's Magic Marker in one hand, the Nerf ball in the other. She tossed him the ball. In large black letters on the spongy surface, she had written the words NIPPER'S BALL.

"Big help you are," said Palmer.

Palmer's nervousness lasted until he went to sleep that night, and resumed when his alarm clock woke him up next morning with the customary nip on the earlobe. He did not feed Nipper on the roof as usual. Instead, he spread newspaper on his floor and poured the Honey Crunchers there, plus some leftover peas from dinner the night before. Nipper loved peas. Then Palmer quickly opened the window and shooed his pigeon into the sky.

Now—what should he wear?

He was afraid that if he wore his usual clothes, Nipper might again recognize him and drop in on him after school. He needed a disguise. He looked around. He found the long-sleeved white shirt that he had once worn to Cousin Linda's wedding, and the dark brown trousers that went with it.

He checked himself in the mirror. He still looked too much like Palmer LaRue. He went down to the basement, to the closet where his mother had stored everyone's winter clothes. He got out his thick, quilted, thigh-length coat, the one his father said could keep him warm at the North Pole. He also grabbed his green woolen stocking cap with the pom-pom and—why not?—his father's black-and-white checkered scarf. He stuffed hat and scarf in his pockets and was sneaking out the door when his mother screeched: "Halt!"

She approached him, squinting as if not believing her eyes. "What's this?" she said, fingering the quilted coat.

"A coat."

"I can see that. It's May. It's warm out."

"I heard it's gonna get colder later on."

"Not that cold."

"Okay, look, I'll unzipper it." He unzippered the coat. "I gotta go, Mom. I'm gonna be late." He bolted down the steps and up the sidewalk, hoping his mother would not call him back. She did not.

In the classroom Palmer kept looking at the clock. For once, he wanted school to last forever. He did not want to walk home. He dreaded the closing bell. When it came he marched up to the teacher and told her he thought she should keep him after school.

She looked at him funny. "And why is that, Palmer?"

"Because I was bad."

She looked surprised. Palmer was never bad. "I was not aware of that."

"You just didn't catch me."

"Is that so? And now you wish to confess?"

"Yes."

"You want to clear your conscience."

"Yes."

"I see." She was smiling. She settled back in her chair. "So, what bad thing did you do?"

"I spit on the floor."

Her eyebrows went up. "Really? Right here? In this room?"

"Yes."

"When did you do this?"

"Uh, after lunch."

She stood. "Would you mind showing me where you did it?"

Palmer had not anticipated this. He had not thought a confession required proof. "I wiped it up," he said.

She nodded, still smiling. "Ah. Well, that was good of you. I think that settles it. You may go on home now."

Palmer stood there, hanging from her eyes. He could not bring himself to go outside. He took a step back, turned to the side and spit on the floor. "Look," he said, "I did it again."

The teacher gasped. She was no longer smiling. He was ordered to fetch a paper towel and clean it up. He was sent to the blackboard to write one hundred times: *I will never never never never never never ever again spit on the floor*. Five of the *nevers* plus the *ever* were his own idea. He wrote as slowly as he could.

The teacher was in and out of the room as he wrote. At one point the guys showed up at the door.

"What're you doing?" Beans asked.

"Being punished," said Palmer.

Beans leaned in to look at the blackboard. "You spit on the *floor?*"

"Yep."

The guys were goggle-eyed.

"Was it a big one?" said Mutto.

"A lunger," said Palmer. The guys were swooning. They were really impressed. "Took me five minutes to clean it up."

At that moment he could have been elected president of the gang.

The teacher returned, and the guys took off. From then on, whenever the teacher left the room or simply wasn't looking, Palmer erased what he had just written. When she finally packed up to go home, she came to the blackboard and counted the sentences. "Nine!" she exclaimed. "Palmer, you write like a snail."

"I'll go faster," he said.

"No, you may stop now. Punishment's over."

Palmer clutched the chalk. "I don't think I should stop till I get to a hundred. I can feel the sentences working. I think I need the whole punishment to make me stop spitting."

The teacher took a step back. The look on her face said: *Is he going to fire one at me?* Then her expression changed, hardened. "Palmer," she said firmly, "I am confident you will never spit in this room again. Now put down the chalk and go home."

He put down the chalk. He got his coat and put it on. He zippered it up. The teacher's jaw dropped, her eyes widened as he pulled the green woolen cap down over his ears, as he wrapped the checkered scarf around his neck and pulled it up to just below his eyes. She was about to say something. "My mother's afraid I'll catch the flu," he blurted and ran from the room before she could stop him.

When he got outside his heart sank: The guys were still there. They had ignored his heavy coat on the way to school, but now, seeing the added scarf and hat, they cracked up.

"Hey Snots, where's the blizzard?"

"You look like Frosty the Snownerd."

"My mom made me," he told them, trying to sound resentful. "She says I'm getting the flu." He tried to steer them to another subject. "What are you doing here, anyway?"

Beans sidled alongside, draped his arm around Palmer's shoulders. "We're your buddies, Snots. You get punished, we wait." His smile was as flat as a cartoon.

"Palmer"—Henry was the only one who occasionally called him by his right name—"be honest, did you *really* spit on the floor?"

Palmer looked them all in the eye. "Yeah. I said, didn't I?"

They weren't sure whether to believe him— but they wanted to, Palmer could tell—and suddenly he realized he had stumbled onto a way to divert attention from Nipper. He marched back to the school door, pulled it open dramatically and pointed inside. He yanked down the scarf and growled. "Go ask Miss Kiner."

They believed. He could see it in their faces. They mobbed him, slapping fives, cheering his name.

On the way home they pestered him again

and again to tell the story, especially the look on the teacher's face. They laughed and thumped his back. They said they didn't think he'd ever do such a thing. They no longer seemed to care, or even notice, that he was muffled up like a mummy.

But they did scan the skies. In the midst of the laughing and thumping, Palmer caught their eyes drifting upward. And Mutto had something new with him this day: a slingshot. Palmer pulled the scarf higher and prayed that Nipper was already home.

27

Nipper was home that day, waiting at the windowsill. But Palmer was too worn out to be relieved. All the stress and weirdness of the day had left him totally wrecked. It was all he could do to drag himself down to dinner.

Summer vacation was over a month away. He couldn't imagine lasting that long.

But he did. Somehow, day by day, he got through it.

Each morning as he left the house he faced two problems, and no matter how well he solved them that day, next morning they would be waiting for him again:

1. How to avoid Nipper on the way home from school.

2. How to keep the guys from turning against him.

As he had discovered the first day, getting into trouble could both detain him after school and boost his popularity with the guys. So he spit on the blackboard, he talked and laughed in class, he took off his shoes and socks, he hid in the map closet, he tickled other students and, on Monday of the last week before summer vacation, he tickled the teacher.

"Palmer!" she shrieked. "What has gotten *into* you?"

She had been asking him this question for some time now. He was running out of answers. "Puberty," he said. He didn't know what it meant, but he had heard that it happened to teenagers and that it made them batty, at least in the eyes of grown-ups.

"Try again," she said. "You're too young for puberty."

"I'm very mature for my age," he said.

"Good," she said, "then you're mature enough to stay after school for a week."

That would take care of the rest of the school year. Palmer forced himself not to grin.

The teacher tickle made Palmer immensely popular, not only with the Beans Boys but throughout the entire school. His reputation soared as a kid who did crazy things. Students broke out laughing when they saw him in the hallways. They egged him on to "do something nutty." They offered him morsels from their lunches.

"You're famous," Dorothy told him in his room one day.

"I know," said Palmer, slumping, "but I don't want to be. I want to be nobody. I want to be invisible. If I was invisible, then Nipper would be too."

Dorothy, for no apparent reason, started to giggle. She quickly clamped her hand over her mouth. "Sorry," she said. "I know I'm not supposed to laugh, but sometimes I can't help it. I keep thinking of you tickling your teacher." Another giggle spouted. "It's just not *you*."

Palmer threw up his hands. "I know! I know! And wait till you see what happens in two days."

Dorothy's eyes widened. "What?"

"Miss Kiner said I won't have detention on the last day of school. I'll have to go home at the regular time. My mom will never let me wear my winter coat anymore in this weather, so I'm afraid Nipper's going to see me again coming home from school." Palmer paced about the room. "I have nightmares all day. I see Nipper

147

landing on my head and Beans snatching him by his legs and—" He couldn't even say the rest. He went over to Nipper, who was strutting along the booktops.

"What are you going to do?" said Dorothy.

Palmer stroked Nipper's smooth, glossy head. "Wear a mask."

Dorothy's hand shot to her mouth. "Oh no."

"Oh yeah." With his fingertips he lightly tickled Nipper's breast feathers. He had discovered that Nipper loved this and would stay still for as long as he kept doing it.

"Do you have a mask?" said Dorothy.

"My elephant mask."

Dorothy screeched, "Your elephant mask? From Halloween? With the trunk?"

"Yeah."

Both of Dorothy's hands clamped her mouth, as if she were about to throw up. Her cheeks flushed, her eyes bulged. She ran from the room and slammed the door. Palmer could hear her muffled sounds coming from the stairway. If he didn't know better, he would have thought she was sobbing.

Minutes later she returned, wiping wetness

from her cheeks, struggling to keep a straight face.

"I'm sorry," she said. She joined Palmer in scratching Nipper's breast feathers.

"I can't wait till school is over," said Palmer.

"I know."

"But I *don't* want it to be over because then it'll be closer to my birthday."

"I know."

"It's all crazy. I almost get dizzy sometimes."

"I know."

Lightly, lazily they tickled Nipper's feathers. Their fingers mingled.

"Know what?" said Dorothy.

"What?"

"You're a hero."

"Huh?"

"All this stuff you're doing. You're probably the naughtiest student there's ever been in our school. And you're doing it all to save him."

Palmer frowned. "That's no hero. I just live in the wrong town, that's all."

The pigeon seemed to be looking at them separately, one with each orange eye. A faint murmur came from deep in his throat.

"Hear that?" said Dorothy. "He's saying,

'That feels *sooooo* good.'"

"Why would anybody want to shoot him?" said Palmer.

"Nobody's going to."

Palmer turned to her. "But why would they *want* to?"

Dorothy stared back. She had no answer.

On the last day of school, wearing his elephant mask on the walk home, the trunk hanging down to his waist, Palmer was a sensation. The problem was keeping the mask on, because first Beans, then everyone else had to yank on the trunk. Every time the mask was pulled off, Palmer covered his face with his hands. He imagined Nipper was circling overhead, trying to spot him.

At last he made it home. He collapsed onto his bed. Nipper marched up one of his legs and down the other. The bird's feet tickled, but Palmer was too worn out to laugh. He could smile, though, for school was over. Finally.

But another school was about to begin.

28

Palmer had just finished supper on Monday when the doorbell rang. It was the guys.

"Let's go," said Beans.

"Where?" said Palmer.

"School. Come on. It starts in ten minutes." Beans grabbed Palmer's wrist and pulled him down the front steps.

Was this some kind of joke?

"School?" said Palmer. "School's over."

"Not this school."

They were trotting. Beans still had his wrist.

Palmer pulled himself free. "What school?" They were heading toward the park. "Where are we going?"

Beans's eyes lit up. "Wringer school."

Palmer felt walloped. He jerked to a halt. Suddenly his throat would not work. He could not speak.

Everyone had stopped.

Beans said, "What's the matter?"

Palmer rasped, "Nothing."

"Ain't you coming to wringer school, Snots?" said Mutto. He was leering.

"Don't you want to learn how to wring pigeons?" said Beans. He moved his fists as if twisting a wet towel. "Don't you want to learn how to wrrrrring their necks?"

Henry was looking away.

Beans was in his face. "You hate pigeons, don't you?"

Palmer nodded. "Sure."

Mutto's eyes were scanning the sky.

Beans thumped his shoulder. "So let's go!"

They ran.

That was the worst of it, the running. What am I doing? Palmer kept thinking, but his legs ran on.

At the soccer field a mob of kids was gathered around a man with a neon pink baseball cap. The man who had been waiting for Palmer for ten years. The wringmaster.

"You stay out of the way," he was saying, calling really, so everyone could hear. "Each shooter gets five shots at a time. Count 'em. Until the last one, you don't move. You stay here." He pointed to the ground at his feet. "Right here. And where are your eyes all this time?"

"On you!" piped half a dozen voices.

The man nodded. "That's right. I'm easy to find, easy to see. I guarantee nobody else is gonna be wearing a hat this ugly."

Giggles.

"So, you're listening for the five shots and watching me, and when I go like this"—he lifted the pink hat and waved it—"that's your signal. You move. Fast. Three of you. We move in groups of three. First man gets the empty bird box and takes it"—he pointed—"over there. So they can load 'er up again with five more birds. The other two, you're moving out onto the field—*fast*. Everything you do is—*fast*." He replaced his hat. He looked over the group. "What's the magic word, men?"

Everyone, including Palmer, yelled: "Fast!"

The man paused, then whispered, "Why?"

For a long time there was no answer. Then a mild, uncertain voice spoke. "There's so many pigeons?"

The man snapped his fingers and pointed to Henry. "Bingo. There's five thousand birds, men, and only one day to turn 'em into fertilizer. Every dead birdie means five bucks to maintain this here park you're standing in.

Anybody here don't play in this park?"

No hands went up.

He shrugged. "There you go. It's for you. You're helping yourself." He looked them over. "Any questions?"

Palmer had a million, but he asked none. Nor did anyone else.

The man nodded. "All right. Last item—wringin' the bird."

A cheer went up from the crowd.

The man held up something.

Another cheer.

The something was gray, perhaps once a large sock. It was stuffed to plumpness, most of it, with a narrow neck ending in a golf ball-size head.

"Stunt pigeon!" someone called out.

Everyone laughed.

The man stared sternly. "Get your giggles over with now. There'll be no giggles on the seven of August. No horsing around. Anybody that's not all business"—he wagged his thumb—"you're outta here. Understand?"

Capped heads nodded.

"Okay, now. The shooter's done. You're a team of three. One of you's gone for the box.

154

The other two—zip—onto the field. What are you gonna find? One of three things. You're either gonna find five dead birds, you're gonna find five floppers—that's what I call the wounded—or you're gonna find—and this'll be most cases—a combination of the above. We got some sorry shooters in this town, and we got some real dead-eyes, but most of 'em are in between."

He raised a finger. "Back up a minute. If wounded birds are floppers, what do you call dead birds?" He looked over the group, his eyes were twinkling.

Someone up front said, "Croakers?"

The wringmaster laughed. "Trick question, son. The answer is dead. Dead is dead. There's no other word for it." He ruffled the kid's hair. "All right . . . you're on the field. Each of you heads for a bird—and not the same bird. No fighting over who gets which bird. This ain't an Easter egg hunt."

Giggles.

"All right. You come to your bird. If it's dead, fine. If it ain't dead, also fine. Whichever, you snatch it up and get the next one. Between the two of you you're coming back with five birds. Here's where you check 'em out. You see one that's not dead"—he swung his head slowly, looking at every face—"you wring its neck."

Palmer heard one stifled squeak; all else was silence.

The man held the gray thing above his head. "One hand here, one hand here, and twist in opposite directions. You do it hard, you do it quick. We're not here to torture these animals. We're here to kill them humanely. Hard and quick. That's all it takes. Into a trash bag. Go to the back of the line. Next time you're up, somebody else gets the box. Keep rotating. Everybody gets a chance. What's the magic word?"

"Fast!"

He looked them over. "Any questions?"

A voice came out of the crowd. "How will we know if it's dead or not?"

Somebody yipped, "Take its pulse!"

The man's glare cut off the laughter.

The trees were silent.

"You'll know," said the man.

The sky was empty.

The man clapped. "All right, line up. This

here's a flopper." He held up the gray stuffed sock. "I want each one of you to step forward, wring it like I showed, and get outta here. I'll see you August seven. Six A.M. sharp. Let's go."

The crowd formed a line. Palmer had notions of drifting away, but Beans and Mutto were herding him their way.

As he waited in line, Palmer felt himself to be four years old again, at his first Family Fest, with the wounded, loppysided pigeon coming toward him and the gray, sour smell of the gun-smoke growing stronger with every breath.

He took his eyes from the field and fixed them on the pink-hatted wringmaster. He noticed how intently the man stared into the face of each kid who stepped up and took the sock. It seemed that the man was on the look-out for pretenders, for kids who didn't really want to be there, for wimps.

And if the man detected a wimp, what would he do? Would he cry out, "Ah-*hah!*" and send the kid away to the jeers of the crowd? Would the kid ever be able to show his face in this town again?

Ahead of him, Beans, then Mutto, wrung the sock. Like most of the kids, they really got into it, grunting with the effort. And now the man was holding it out to Palmer. Palmer accepted it.

Beans's voice came from nearby. "Wring it, Snots."

Palmer could feel the man's eyes on him. He wondered how his face looked. Would the man say, "Ah-*hah!*"?

Palmer had half expected the sock to sprout pink feet and glossy feathers. It did not. He wanted to call out to all the wringers-in-training: *Hey, who are they trying to kid? This is no pigeon. You want to know what a real pigeon feels like—ask me. This is nothing but a sock.*

"Let's go, son," said the man. "Hard and quick."

Palmer wrung its neck, hard and quick. He dashed it to the ground at the man's feet and marched off.

The man said nothing.

Palmer caught the weightless, foamy basketball. He turned it in his hands to look at Nipper's name in broad marker strokes. He tossed the ball back to Dorothy. Nipper chuckled down at them from a curtain rod.

"If it was only a sock," said Dorothy, "why do you keep worrying about it?"

Palmer got up and paced back and forth. "I'm worrying because in thirteen days I'm going to be ten. And twenty-eight days after that is Family Fest. And then it won't be a sock anymore."

No one spoke for a while. Nipper flew to the basket rim. Palmer paced.

At last Dorothy said, "Tell them."

Palmer looked at her. "Huh?"

"Tell them."

"Tell them what?"

"You don't want to be a wringer. You're *not* going to be a wringer."

Palmer stared. "Tell who?"

Dorothy stared back. Suddenly a huge grin broke across her face, she threw out her arms. "Everybody!"

Palmer glared at her. He sneered, "Yeah, right."

Dorothy jumped down from her usual perch on Palmer's desk. "Okay then," she said, "how about if *I* tell them?" She bolted for the window. She threw up the screen, leaned out over the porch roof and yelled, "Hey, everybody, I have an announcement!"

Palmer yanked her back into the room and slammed down the screen. He stood redfaced, fuming. Dorothy wiggled and giggled out of his grasp and went to play with Nipper. Palmer shut the window and locked it. He pulled down the shade. But he could not shut out the cold, wet feeling that he had just peeked into his future.

When he turned back to Dorothy, he found her wearing an impish grin. "So," she said, "are you going to invite me to your birthday party this year?"

Palmer sagged. He had been dreading this. So far his social life had been neatly divided into two separate relationships: one with

Dorothy, one with the guys. Dorothy herself helped keep it that way by avoiding him whenever the guys were around.

Last year, except for his mother's complaint, it had been fairly easy not to invite Dorothy. This year was hugely different. Dorothy was now his best friend, the only person in the world with whom he shared Nipper. How could he not invite her?

And how could he not invite the guys?

"Well?" said Dorothy.

"Maybe I won't even have a party," he said.

But he knew he would. Because the guys were already talking about it. They were expecting it. And because his strategy for surviving the summer was simply this: stay on their good side.

It was becoming harder and harder to do, for in these recent weeks Palmer had come to realize that, with the possible exception of Henry, the guys whose company he had once craved he now feared. If they ever found out for sure that he was a traitor, Farquar's Treatment would feel like baby's play compared to what they could do. He imagined them torturing him until he led them to his forbidden pet. At that point Nipper was as good as dead.

So when his mother at dinner one day said, "Do you want a party this year?" Palmer's answer was yes.

After a long pause, his mother said, "Okay, but you have to invite Dorothy too."

Palmer just shrugged and nodded. Sometimes the effort of getting through each day left him feeling heavy and dopey by dinnertime. He wished he could just go to bed and not wake up until September.

And then his mother, sprinkling salt on a baked potato, said ever so casually, "You don't happen to know anyone looking for a lost cat, do you?"

Instantly Palmer was alert. "No, why?"

"Oh," she said, "I've noticed one around the last few days."

Did a spider just walk across his shoulders?

"Around where?"

"Backyard. Around the side. That was yesterday. Today I found it inside, on the stairway."

Palmer's heart pounded in his chest. "What color?"

"Yellow," she said, reaching for the pepper.

She said more but he was not hearing. He was racing upstairs, bursting into his room, finding Nipper healthy and plump and waddling across the floor to meet him. He fell to his knees and pounded his fist again and again into his thigh.

3O

Although she insisted that she would be there right up to the last minute, Dorothy did not come to Palmer's birthday party. Neither did his mother. "I'll leave your father to deal with your hoodlum friends this year," she said, and went off shopping.

The guys were thrilled. They had learned about the Sharpshooter Award, and to them Palmer's father was as big a hero as a battlefield general. They kept running back to the den to look at and touch the trophy.

They flung questions:

"Is it real gold, Mr. LaRue?"

"How many pigeons did you shoot?"

"Can we see your gun?"

At the dining room table Beans gave a speech about himself, about his hatred of pigeons and how many necks he intended to wring. He called to Palmer's father, who was in the kitchen planting candles in the cake. "I bet you hate them dirty birds even more than me, don't you, Mr. LaRue?"

Palmer's father came to the doorway. He looked directly at Beans. He smiled. "No," he said, "I don't hate pigeons. Never did." He returned to the cake.

The empty look on Beans's face indicated that the answer had reached his ears, but no farther. He called, "You were a wringer, right, Mr. LaRue?"

"I was."

"And now Snots is too, huh? How about that?" The reply from the kitchen came after a long pause. "Palmer decides for himself. It's up to him."

Palmer gaped at the doorway as Beans thumped his fist on the table and growled, "Where's the grub?"

Like everyone else, Palmer ate his ice cream and cake, but he wasn't hungry. He opened his presents but did not enjoy them. On this day that he had dreaded for so long, he had no appetite for anything.

As everyone belted out "Happy Birthday," Palmer stared at the man marching in with the cake and tried to imagine him pulling the trigger again and again as gray-feathered Nippers fell from the sky. The cake was placed in front of him, and Palmer found that he could neither move nor breathe. The heat from the ten tiny fires burned his face. In the plump, shimmering shapes of the candle flames he saw the ghosts of ten pigeons. "Blow 'em out!" someone squawked.

Palmer squeezed his eyes shut and blew them out.

Outside after the party, they went in search of Farquar. When Palmer recalled last year's Treatment, he could hardly believe his own memory: pride, honor, little kids lining up to touch his devastated arm. True, last year he felt the same terror that he felt now, but he knew that after Farquar's ten knuckles this year, no pride, no honor awaited him. Only pain and uselessness.

To his great relief, they could not find Farquar.

At dinnertime the boys split up, and Palmer returned home alone. He fed and played with Nipper. He did not feed himself. He received a happy birthday phone call from Dorothy.

Dusk was falling outside when a twinge of hunger sent him to the kitchen. He found the leftover half cake covered and sitting atop the refrigerator. He got it down. He set it on the table. He lifted the cover—and gasped aloud. Finger-lettered in the chocolate icing along the side of the two-layer cake was a single word:

TONIGHT

31

Henry.

Thinking back, Palmer recalled that as the gang was leaving the house that afternoon, Henry had rushed back in, claiming he had forgotten something.

Henry.

Whose streak, unlike Beans's, was meek, not mean.

Who ran with Beans and Mutto. Who did what they did. But was different.

Who Palmer had seen one day pulling his little sister around the block in a wagon.

Henry had done it. Fingered the word into the icing.

Tonight.

It was a warning. Something was going to happen tonight. Something not good.

But what?

As he smeared over the word with a dinner knife, Palmer thought about it. The only place he would be at night would be in his room, in bed. If something bad were going to happen to him, that's where it would have to be.

It must have something to do with Beans and Mutto. Or the cat. The cat had already been slipped into the house. Maybe this time— tonight—they would slip themselves in. They had already done so once. And lately, Beans especially had taken an interest in Palmer's room. Palmer, acting put out with his parents, kept insisting he was not allowed to have visitors upstairs. This, however, had not prevented Beans from climbing the stairs to the bathroom no fewer than three times during the party.

Palmer considered phoning Henry to ask him directly, but that felt risky. Left to his best guess, he decided the warning meant that he was to have visitors that night. Considering the guys' recent suspicions, it did not take a genius to figure out that the purpose of the visit had to do with a certain feathered roommate.

He went upstairs to feed Nipper, who had returned from his daily wanderings. While the pigeon pecked at nacho pieces, Palmer sat on the bed to think the whole thing through. It occurred to him that he could close and lock his window and thus keep them out. It was a simple solution, but it also created its own problems. The guys might keep banging on the window all night until Palmer answered. Foiled at Palmer's window, they might get in other ways, other windows. They might wake up his parents. And most important, with the window closed on a hot summer night and no one answering their taps on the pane, they might well become more suspicious than ever.

No, the window had to stay open. He had to let them in. And that meant, of course, that Nipper could not be in the room. Neither could Palmer. He thought about it. They would go downstairs. They would hide in the dark. He did not think the guys would search the whole house. The target was his bedroom.

And what could he say next day when Beans asked him where he was last night? He could say it was too hot in his room so he slept downstairs on the sofa. Or, even better, he stayed overnight at relatives'.

The moon was beaming outside his window when a happy thought came to him: this whole thing could turn in his favor. Once they saw for themselves that there was no pigeon or evidence of a pigeon, they might drop their suspicions. They might believe him. They might back off. So maybe, crazy as it sounded, it was good that they were coming.

Palmer had no trouble staying awake in the dark. He was too nervous to sleep. At last he heard his parents' footsteps coming up the stairs. Ten minutes later the bright crack under his bedroom door went dark.

He waited until he thought they were asleep. He turned on the flashlight he had brought up for this night. Nipper up was at his usual spot on the closet shelf. When the light beam struck, the eye facing Palmer went from buttonhole slit to orange button; otherwise the bird did not move. This was normal behavior, Palmer knew. Nipper would be easy to handle. When he settled down to roost, he went into a dopey trance that firecrackers could not disturb.

Palmer stood on a chair and, cupping his hands, gently lifted his forbidden pet from the shelf. Holding both pigeon and flashlight was tricky, but Palmer managed to tiptoe downstairs without waking up the house. At first he sat on the sofa, with Nipper in his lap. Still feeling unsafe, he went behind the sofa. He turned off the flashlight.

In the utter darkness he felt himself to be nothing but ears and fingertips. He could feel Nipper's heartbeat, putt-putting away behind the toothpick ribs like a tiny motor scooter. He could feel the cold, golden gaze of the trophy pigeon two rooms away. The silence of the house at night was not total. Somewhere a clock was ticking. Cricks and creaks came from nearby and distant quarters, as if the house were twitching in a sleep of its own.

Palmer tried to aim his hearing upstairs. He held his breath as long as he could, listening. Was that a window screen opening? A footstep? He pictured them in his room, shadows, dark upon dark, Beans's penlight like a starflake moving in the darkness, pointing at the bed— *He's not here!*—pointing under the bed, shining · on the bookcase, the basket rim, the desk, the closet . . . the closet shelf . . . the empty closet shelf . . . the closet . . . *oh no!* . . . the closet *floor . . . the Honey Crunchers!* He had forgotten to bring them downstairs. Would they see them? Would they figure the cereal was Palmer's, for snacking? Or would they guess the real reason?

He thought of going up—because maybe they were *not* there—racing up the stairs, grabbing the cereal box, racing back down. Ten seconds was all he needed. He could do it. But what if they *were* there? What if that creak he just heard . . .

He stayed put. He crouched and cringed behind the sofa as if neither furniture nor darkness were enough to hide him. He stayed through a thousand tocks of the unseen clock, and another thousand, and the bonging of his heart. And only when he heard, from behind the house, two sharp, quick yelps, did he know for absolutely sure that they had been there.

And even then he waited for another thousand tocks before he allowed himself a deep breath and, at last, sleep.

32

He awoke to Nipper pecking at his ear. And just in time. His father, earliest bird in the house, was coming down the stairs. He scooped up his pigeon and crouched behind the sofa. When his father passed into the kitchen, he dashed up the steps and into his room.

Glancing around, he saw no evidence of night visitors. The window screen was firmly shut. Everything was in its place.

Except one thing, as he soon found out.

He hadn't even had breakfast yet when the doorbell rang. As soon as he opened the door he found himself facing the Nerf basketball. Curling around it were Beans's fingers.

"Who's Nipper?"

Palmer could not think fast enough.

Beans pressed the ball into Palmer's nose. "Who wrote this?"

He did not want to get Dorothy involved. "I did," he said.

"So who is Nipper?"

Palmer blurted the first thing that came to mind. "Me. It used to be my nickname when I was little." He looked at them all. "Before I knew you guys."

Mutto stepped up beside Beans. "We think Nipper's a pigeon."

Palmer made a shocked face. "Pigeon? What would I do with a pigeon?"

"What would you do with that cereal and nachos you got in your room?" said Beans.

Palmer laughed, showing them how wrong they were. "Snacks. I keep stuff in my room so I don't have to go all the way down to the kitchen." He wanted to kick himself for forgetting about Nipper's food.

"And where were you last night?" said Beans.

It occurred to Palmer that he had a right to questions of his own. "Where was *I*? Where were *you*?" He glanced at Henry. Henry's face showed nothing. "Where did you get my ball?"

Beans grinned. "We came to see you last night."

"You weren't there," said Mutto.

Palmer nodded. "I know. I was sleeping overnight at somebody's. My cousin's. I wasn't here."

Henry was staring at the sky. Palmer saw Henry for what he was: a captive, strong enough to warn him about last night, but too weak to do anything except follow Beans. He saw in Henry something of himself, and worse, what he could become.

Beans scowled at the ball, at Palmer. "You ain't Nipper. You're Snots." He dropped the ball to the ground and stepped on it. When he raised his foot, the foam ball reclaimed its roundness. Beans cursed and stomped on the ball with both feet, flattening it, grinding it into the sidewalk. For a full minute he grunted with the effort, and again the ball popped back to shape. He kicked it away. He yanked on Palmer's arm. "Let's go. We gotta find Farquar."

They found Farquar in front of the deli, eating chocolate cupcakes and drinking Coke.

Beans announced, pointing to Palmer: "Birthday boy. Ten years old."

Slouched against the deli window, Farquar took a swig of Coke. He swished it around in his mouth. He raised his upper lip, giving himself a rodentlike face, and spit a thin stream of

Coke between his front teeth. The boys shot backward.

Farquar peered at Palmer. "Wringer, huh?"

Palmer did not answer.

"He needs The Treatment," said Beans.

Farquar glared. "You rushing me?"

Beans spread his arms. "No. I'm just sayin'."

Farquar bit a cupcake in half. Chocolate icing covered his teeth. "What's it look like I'm doin'?"

"Eatin'?" replied Beans tentatively.

"Eatin' breakfast," said Farquar, washing down his mouthful with Coke. The boys took another step back. "You don't say nothin' while I'm eatin' breakfast. Y'understand?"

All four boys nodded. They retreated to the curb and sat down, facing the street, not daring to even look at Farquar.

After a long time they heard his voice: "Okay." They turned. He was walking up the sidewalk. They got up and followed. He turned into an airshaft between two storefronts and went back to the alley. He stopped. He backed away from them, making space. All faces were grim. No one spoke.

Farquar pointed to the ground in front of

him. He looked into Palmer's eyes. "Step up."

Palmer stepped up.

"Right or left."

"Left."

"Roll it up."

He rolled his left sleeve up to the shoulder. He blinked several times. He looked around. He rolled his sleeve back down. He took a step back. He shook his head.

Farquar's brow pinched in surprise. "What?"

"No," said Palmer. The word came out choked and dry.

"No?" said Farquar. A chocolate crumb was wedged between his front teeth.

"No," said Palmer, clearly this time. He heard shuffling behind him.

"No what?"

No what?

Palmer moved, away from them all, facing them all.

They stared at him, waiting. He saw the foot grinding the ball, the name into the sidewalk. He heard the scream, heard it coming a split second before the others heard it, the scream that he knew now had been growing inside him for a long time. He planted his feet and bent his knees and balled his fists and let it come all the way out: "No nothing! No Treatment! No wringer! No Snots!" He thrust his scream at Beans. "I'm not Snots! My name is Palmer! My name is Palmer!" He stepped back, he hunkered down. "No!"

Then he ran.

Down the alleys, down the streets, he ran like he had never run before. If Farquar was with them, he would be caught, he knew that. But if not, he might be able to outrun the guys. He heard their sneakers slapping the pavement behind him. He heard their calls.

"You're dead meat, Snots!"

"I'm gonna eat that pigeon a' yours!"

"I'm gonna wring its neck and pull its head off!"

"I'm pullin' *yer* head off!"

He ran and ran.

33

A bug crawled down the middle of his back. He tried to reach it. He whipped off his shirt, ran a fingertip up his spine. It wasn't a bug. It was sweat.

The sun boiled in a cloudless sky. The Dumpster had been slowly reeling in its shadow, so that he now had to sit with his back flat against it and his knees drawn up in order to remain wholly in the shade. The Dumpster's metal flank felt cool and crusty against his bare back.

His breath and heartbeat had long since returned to normal. The noontime music of church bells had passed an hour ago, maybe two. He was hungry, thirsty. But also safe. The only other safe place being his own house, which was exactly five and a half blocks from this Dumpster behind the GreatGrocer super-market.

A back door slammed open. Out came a worker dragging two hugely swollen black plastic bags. Seeing Palmer, he said, "You waiting to help me?"

Was the man joking? He wasn't smiling. "No," answered Palmer.

With a grunt the worker heaved one bag, then the other into the Dumpster. He looked down at Palmer. He wagged his head. "Made in the shade." He went back inside.

Five and a half blocks. In his head Palmer plotted a course that, except for the final half block, kept him in alleyways. Even so, streets would have to be crossed, in broad daylight. And anyway, the guys themselves took alleys as often as streets. They could be anywhere, around any corner, behind any parked car. They could be in front of the GreatGrocer right now, asking people, "Did you see a kid . . . ?" They might already be spreading word around town. "Palmer LaRue has a pigeon." He knew that if that fact had ever been in question, the question had been answered spectacularly by his actions of the morning.

The back door slammed open. The worker came out, but this time there was nothing in his hands but a can of Sprite. He stopped in front of Palmer and held the can down to him. It hadn't been opened. "You look like you need this, kid."

It occurred to Palmer that this might be some kind of trick. But he was too thirsty to care. He took the can. It felt blessedly cold. He stared up at the man. He felt like crying. The man's lips almost smiled. "On the house," he said, and he was gone.

Palmer snapped open the Sprite and drank the can empty, taking time out only to gasp for breath. He lay his head back against the Dumpster and closed his eyes. In spite of himself, in spite of everything, for a precious few seconds he felt good.

His first idea had been to wait until dark, then make a run for home. As the sun dropped below the roofline of the GreatGrocer, he began to see that the idea was bad. Nipper would be coming home soon, and who could say that they were not waiting for him? Maybe even on the porch roof itself, with stones, slingshots. Suddenly it was clear: He had to get home before Nipper.

Now.

He dropped the can and ran.

Alley and street, he took the fastest way, driven by images of Nipper flying into a blizzard of stones. As he approached the turn onto his block, it occurred to him that they might be waiting at his front door. It occurred to him that this might be his last minute on earth. He slowed down. And thought of Nipper. And ran on. They were not there. He burst into his house.

He wanted to collapse right then and there, to rub his face in the living-room rug, but he dared not stop. He took the stairs three at a time, flung open the door. Nipper was at the window, on the sill outside the screen, and inside, sitting on his pillow, was the yellow cat Panther, facing the window, its head as still as a statue, its tail sweeping slowly from side to side. It hadn't even bothered to look at Palmer.

The closest thing was a comic book. Palmer hurled it. The cat hissed, screeched, leaped to the floor and was downstairs before Palmer finished his scream.

It was then, as he opened the screen to let Nipper in, that he knew his pigeon must go.

34

Dorothy was crying.

"Why tomorrow?"

"Because they know," he said for the third time. He pounded the bed. "They know, they know, they know. And they're not gonna wait. Plus Pigeon Day is coming up. It's only gonna get worse."

"Henry wouldn't hurt Nipper."

"Henry doesn't count. It's the others."

She implored. "But *why*? Why can't you just hide him in the house? Or in my house?"

"They'll find out." He spoke wearily, pacing. "They were right in this room last night. The cat was here today. They know everything. They won't give up. What we really ought to do is take him out tonight, under cover of darkness."

She blurted, "No!"

"So," he shrugged, "tomorrow."

She slumped facing the wall, her forehead leaning into it. "Why don't they just let him alone?" She looked at him as if the answer were his to reveal. "What did he ever do to them?"

He looked up to the closet shelf, where Nipper was roosting. "He was born a pigeon, that's what."

"But how can you *do* it?" she whined.

The months of spring and summer had filed his nerves to a point. He was nearly galloping back and forth across his room. Though he muffled the volume of his voice, lest his parents hear, his entire body screamed, "How can I *do* it? How can I *do* it? Can't you get it through your head? They're gonna *kill* him! Do you want him *dead?*"

Earlier in the day Dorothy had seen the unflattenable Nerf ball in the street and had retrieved it. She stroked it now in her lap. Her voice was barely audible. "I just don't want him gone."

He went to the window. A quarter moon was out. He began to weep. "Do you think I do?"

The next morning they met at six o'clock, with bikes. Dorothy's bike had a wicker basket fixed to the handlebars. That's where the shoe box went. Palmer had dumped the toy soldiers onto the bed, poked air holes in the lid and deposited the pigeon.

They had told their parents that they were going on an early-morning breakfast picnic to the park. In the basket also lay a box of donuts and mini-cartons of iced tea.

They rode to the park, and out of the park, and out of town. They rode past the barbecue restaurant and the burnt-out barn and the golf course, whose dew-topped greens looked like silver ponds. They stopped only to switch bikes when Dorothy could no longer bear to transport the basket. They pedaled down roads they had seen only from a car before, and then down roads they had never seen at all. The only sounds were the whir of spokes, the crunch of tires. Up and down hills they rode and rode until it seemed they must be in another state, if not another country.

Palmer, leading the way, pulled off the road by a field where horses were grazing.

"Let's eat," he said.

Dorothy took the donuts and drinks from the bike basket. "Is this where we let him go?"

"No. Not far enough."

"Not *far* enough?"

He punched a straw into an iced tea carton and took a long sip. He shook his head. "We have to go as far as we can. Pigeons can find their way back from a long way off."

Dorothy broke off a piece of donut and stuck it under the lid of the shoe box. It was immediately snatched from her fingers. "*I* can't even find my way back from here."

"You're not a pigeon." He bit into a donut. "Even far's not enough. It has to be confusing too."

She was alarmed. "What do you mean? You're not going to blindfold him?"

He sneered. "No. But something else. You'll see." He had taken only one bite of the donut. He slipped the rest into the shoe box. "Let's go."

Another endless stretch of riding brought them to an unfenced meadow. Palmer said, "Here," and veered into it. "Wait," he called back.

Dorothy stopped at the roadside and watched Palmer drive her bicycle deeper into the meadow. The wheels jumped, the basket bounced over the clodded earth. Thistletops erupted, wildflowers wobbled as the bike charged in reckless patterns only a fly could follow: circles, figure eights, zigzags, crazy doodles. This went on for many minutes when suddenly the bike bolted on a beeline into the woods beyond.

Dorothy waited as long as she could before becoming impatient, then worried. She could not see an inch into the dense treeline. The sun was directly overhead, making a shadowless desert of the meadow. The handlebars of the bicycle were hot. Then, there he was, popping from the woods, pedaling furiously straight at her, the donut box flying in the basket. As he came closer she saw that his face was red and wet, his mouth twisted. The shoe box was empty. He did not stop nor look at her, but charged with a clatter onto the road.

It was a long time before he slowed down, allowing her to catch up. They switched back to their own bikes. They rode in silence. They asked directions at a gas station. They bought sodas and threw away the donuts. When they coasted the final hill into town, the streets were in shadow. Wearily they climbed the stairs to Palmer's room. Nipper was waiting on the windowsill.

35

He thought of not feeding Nipper. Of not letting him in. Sooner or later the pigeon would get the hint and fly away forever. He told Dorothy of his idea, hoping she would forbid it. She did. She yelped so loud he had to clamp his hand over her mouth.

"Okay, o-*kay*," he said. He began pacing. "But we have to do something. We gotta get rid of him."

Dorothy did not argue.

"They're not gonna give up. No way. Not till they get him."

Pacing, pacing.

"They're gonna keep sneaking the cat in. They're gonna spy on the house. Day and night. Day and night. They'll wait and wait. Slingshots. BB guns. Maybe even poison. Poison!"

Pacing. Arms upthrust.

"They'll put poisoned cereal on the roof!"

Dorothy was laughing.

Palmer stopped, scowled. "What?"

She was on her back on the bed, on the toy soldiers, howling at the ceiling. She dragged herself up, found her voice. "Do what you were doing."

"What?"

"Walk."

He took a step.

"No no. *Walk.*" She swept her hand. "Back and forth, like you were."

He resumed pacing, suddenly conscious of his feet. He looked down—and saw what she was laughing at. Nipper was pacing, turning when he turned, tracing his every move back and forth across his room.

He halted. The pigeon halted. He didn't know whether to laugh or cry.

The next day his mother confessed.

It happened after breakfast. He was in his room. He heard his mother's footsteps coming up the stairs. Normally the footsteps would turn and head for the bathroom or her own bedroom. This time they came straight to his door.

She knocked. "Palmer? Can I come in?"

Quickly he glanced about the room. He noted two white powdery droppings that he had neglected to clean up. And a cereal box on the floor. He had been getting lax lately. At least the bird itself had left for the day. He kicked the cereal box under the bed. He composed his face.

"Come in."

She came in smiling. "Hi," she said. She waved, as if she hadn't seen him in the kitchen two minutes ago.

"Hi," he said. He did not wave. He was standing on one of the powdery poopies. The other was on his desk. Which was exactly where she sat, her left hand, palm down, no more than an inch from the white deposit.

He expected her to look around, to inspect the place that she had been asked to stay away from for months now. But she kept looking only at him, smiling, and he saw now that it was not quite her regular smile. There was a goofy quality to it, it was changing, breaking down.

"I have a confession to make," she said. Her face was sad now, droopy; but it wasn't real, it was pretend, clownish.

He said nothing.

The smile was back, real and regular. "We know you have a pigeon."

He could not move or speak.

She laughed. "Palmer—breathe."

He breathed.

She held out her arms. "Come here." He went to her and was swallowed entirely in her embrace. All strength drained out of him, and all of a sudden he understood how alone he had been and how much he had missed his parents' support. He sobbed. She held him tighter, swaying.

From beyond her heartbeat he heard her voice.

"Didn't you notice things weren't always the way you left them? Didn't you notice that it never got dusty in here? Did you really think you could keep your mother out of a room in her own house?"

Actually, yes, he had thought so.

She held him at arm's length. He had never seen such a smile. Her eyes were gleaming, radiant. "Didn't you notice that a new box of Honey Crunchers magically appeared in your closet whenever the old box was almost empty?"

He stared at her, blinking. Yes, he had noticed, and that's exactly what he had thought: magic.

She laughed aloud, hugged him again, released him.

"Did you think you could have a pet pigeon in the house since—what?—January, and Daddy and I wouldn't know about it?"

"I thought you'd be mad," he said.

She fluttered her fingers at the door. "Go get me a tissue." He fetched a tissue from her room. She used it to wipe the dropping from the desk. "And don't forget the one you're standing on," she said, tossing the tissue into the basket. She stared at him. "Mad? Why would we be mad at you?"

He stated the obvious: "It's a *pigeon*."

She nodded. Her voice became even softer. "I understand. We understand. And we were a little concerned, but not mad. Never mad."

"But—" He did not know how to put it. "Dad."

She smiled. "Don't worry. Your dad's been changing. He didn't even go to watch Pigeon Day last year, much less shoot." She put a hand on his shoulder. "One night—don't tell him I told you this—one night he snuck into your room while you were sleeping and stood there with a flashlight at your closet looking at your pigeon." She chuckled. "Take my word for it, that bird is as safe with your dad as it is with you."

They talked through much of the morning. Palmer told her everything. Nipper's arrival after the snowstorm. The daily wake-up ear peck. The guys and their growing suspicions. Treestumping Dorothy. Spitting on the class-room floor. (He wished he had a camera to pre-serve the look on her face.) Refusing The Treatment. When he told her of his lifelong fear, that he dreaded the day he would become ten and a wringer, his lip quivered and she made a sound of pain and squeezed him tight to her and stroked his head and his back.

After a while she said, "Don't let Nipper go. Keep him."

He tried to explain. He tried to make her understand what life was like for him. That there was simply was not enough room in town, not this town, for himself, the guys and a pigeon. His fear was too great, he told her, and his course had been set.

So when, a day later, Dorothy told him that her family was heading to the seashore for a vacation, Palmer asked her to take Nipper along and release him there. She protested, but in the end she spoke to her parents, and her parents, as Palmer had hoped they would, agreed to take care of things.

Dorothy came for Nipper the night before. She refused to use the shoe box. She carried the sleeping bird across the street in her hands. The next day Palmer stayed in bed until noon.

36

Despite the heat, he slept with his window shut and locked, the shade drawn. Still he could hear them, Beans and Mutto squalling like alleycats on the back porch roof. He could hear them raise the screen, knock on the window, work to open it.

On the street they treestumped him. They planted themselves in front of him so that he had to step around them, only to find them replanted in his new path. It took him half an hour to walk one block. They mocked and taunted him. They flicked his ears and spit on his sneakers. Beans bared his green-and-yellow teeth and breathed baked beans into his face.

It was as if he had never been one of them.

"He's gone," he told them.

They laughed. They didn't believe him.

He had an idea. Invite them into his room, let them see for themselves. Maybe then they would believe, back off. But then he realized that his mother would never again allow them into her house. It then occurred to him that when he thought of the guys he was really thinking only of two of them: Beans and Mutto. Not Henry. Henry was one of them, all right, but he was different. Maybe he could sneak Henry into his room, prove it to Henry.

The guys agreed. He did not have to convince Beans and Mutto that his mother was dangerous to them, especially in her house. And while it frustrated them that only Henry would have the privilege, they were too curious not to let it happen.

Beans looked up at Henry. He tugged on Henry's red-and-white-striped T-shirt until Henry bent down to Beans's height. "Check it out good. Don't let him trick ya."

Henry nodded.

"Report back to me."

"Okay."

Palmer chose a morning when his mother was out. While Beans and Mutto waited, sitting brazenly across the street on Dorothy's front steps, he led Henry into his house. Up in the room he held out both arms and said, "It's all yours. Look all you want."

While Henry looked about, poking obediently into the closet, Palmer studied Henry.

Henry was so tall that the top of his head grazed the basketball net. And yet, somehow, he did not give an impression of bigness. On the contrary, he seemed quite small, smaller than Beans and Mutto, smaller even than Palmer.

"Thanks for the warning," Palmer said to him.

Henry, peering foolishly into the wastebasket, said, "What warning?"

"On the cake."

Henry paused, then said, "Oh. Yeah."

Palmer watched him search some more.

"What's your real name?"

Henry looked startled. His eyes went to the window, as if the guys might be lurking there. He never looked at Palmer. "Huh?"

"I know Beans's real name is Arthur. And Mutto is Billy. Who are you, really?"

Henry dropped to his knees and ducked under the bed. He stood back up. His wide, startled eyes, careful to avoid Palmer, swept across the walls. "George," he said and left the room. He hurried down the stairs.

Palmer called, "George! Quit!" He called, "I saw you pulling your little sister in the wagon!"

But Henry Really George was already out the door.

37

Whatever Henry told them they must have believed, for they backed off. If they came across Palmer in the street or at the park, they continued to harass him. But they stopped coming to his house. They did not go out of their way to find him.

Not that he cared.

He tumbled lifelessly through July, feeling as dry and empty as the cicada husks on the trees. Down empty alleyways he rode his bike.

He hardly ever saw Dorothy. They avoided each other. When they met accidentally on the street, they said hi and quickly turned in opposite directions.

He threw away the shoe box that had served as both the soldiers' barracks and Nipper's roost. He kept the soldiers in his sock drawer. Sometimes he took them out to play. He arranged them on his desk, facing them to the enemy. Sometimes the enemy was large and formidable, such as a hippo slipper; sometimes it was one pink, defenseless eraser.

One day his father showed him the proper placement of the troops. How to space them out, so that a land mine would never kill more than one. How to send flankers to the left and right, curling in a semicircle to hit the enemy from three sides and prevent him from sneaking behind you. How to keep a platoon in reserve. He learned where to place the green-faced lieutenant and the captain, and, high ground being priceless, to set the machine gunner on a book, a children's dictionary.

Usually it came to no more than this: a deployment of troops, twenty-seven soldiers leaning, twenty-seven tiny olive-green rifles aiming, poised on the brink of battle. And then one day they attacked. They moved forward, they bore down on the eraser from three sides, cutting off all retreat, pinning it down in murderous crossfire, the lieutenant leading the charge, the captain shouting commands, calling in air strikes. Yet somehow the wicked eraser managed to stay alive, managed even to crawl through the front lines, only to be greeted by the backup platoon. Amazingly, it survived this as well and was up and running and thought itself home free—when the machine gun opened up from atop the dictionary. RATATATATAT-ATATATATATAT. A merciless fusillade the machine gun laid down, and the troops regrouped and joined the fire and the roar of war did not cease until the eraser was dead and cut to ribbons.

The next day he buried the soldiers in the backyard. The tiny green faces said nothing, the tiny green eyes stared up at him as the dirt fell upon them.

He continued to read Beetle Bailey and to cut out the strips, but he no longer mounted them in his collection. Then he stopped cutting them out. Then he stopped reading.

He never touched the Nerf ball. The net hung unswished.

He still kept his door closed, but sometimes he kept it open too.

He went with his father to a Titans baseball game, in the twilight semipro league. They drove to Denville. It was good to go to another town. But not very good. He ate a hot dog with relish and a soft pretzel with mustard and a birch beer. The birch beer was red. The uniforms of the Titans were orange. The shirts were orange, and the socks and the T on the cap. A black-and-orange stripe went from the belt to the top of the stirruped sock. The catcher's chest protector was orange, and so were the shortstop's shoelaces.

In the fourth inning there was a home run, then another, greater one. The ball flew high above the cheering crowd into the twilight sky, over the billboarded fence. It landed in dirt beyond the centerfielder's leap and rolled onto the parking lot, a white pureness against the black macadam. Suddenly kids were racing, a flock of boys bending themselves around parked cars, colliding at the rolling ball. When they separated, one hand was raised.

In the last inning there was a foul ball, though at first Palmer did not know it. He was reading the billboards when suddenly the people around him were leaping from their seats, someone was shouting, "Look out!" A shadow fell over him. Turning, he heard the sound, inches from his face—something like a slap— then laughter, his father's voice saying "Gotcha!"; his father's body standing, leaning over him, blotting out the entire field and sky. Then the light came back and someone was saying "Look at his face," and his father was smiling and looking down, and his hands were opening like a flower.

On the ride home Palmer held the foul ball in his own hands. He imagined he felt a heartbeat.

38

It was as if he could smell into the future. The gray, sour odor of gunsmoke came to him a full week before Family Fest was due to begin. There were shots too: the popping of cap pistols from four- and five-year-olds practicing to one day be wringers and shooters. All things in their gun-sights became pigeons: grasshoppers, mailboxes, yellow squash, each other.

The sun dazzled in a cloudless sky. The side-walks, if you took your shoes off, burned. After dinner people watered flowers.

At night he heard trucks rumbling.

Little kids on pastel bikes pedaled furiously, churning the heat to butter, gasping stories of wooden crates piled higher than skyscrapers, of crates broken into, pigeons flushed and killed, security guards posted.

Men on porches cleaned their shotguns.

Women baked pies.

In the mornings he thought he felt a nip on his ear. He opened his eyes and looked about, but he was alone.

At first Palmer believed he had released Nipper for Nipper's sake. Then he began to see that it had been for his own sake as well. He knew this from the relief he felt from sleeping with the window open, of no longer fearing the yellow cat. The tension that had choked him for months was gone.

The price of peace had been high: expelling himself from the gang, proclaiming himself a traitor, banishing his beloved pet. For such a price, a peace should be excellent. Yet when Palmer reached for it, tried to taste it, it was not there. Instead he found only his blizzard-blown friend—images and memories and dreams.

One night he dreamed about a pigeon crossing a road in a faraway place. A car zoomed by, knocking the pigeon down. Other cars zoomed, and soon the pigeon was meat and feathers, flat. Then an old woman with a watering can began to sprinkle the road, and the meat plumped up and came together again with the feathers, and the old woman took the reconstituted pigeon in her hands—only now it wasn't an old woman, it was a kid, a wringer, throttling the pigeon by the neck, and the pigeon had a beak that was

soft like lips and the pigeon was speaking . . .
speaking. . . .

Throughout the days and nights of Family Fest,
he stayed close to his parents. He did the Fun
House with his father and Tilt-A-Whirl with
his mother. Several times in the noise and jos-
tle he thought he heard Beans's voice. At the
bake sale he had never seen so many pies at
once, more pies on the endless table than soldiers buried in his backyard. His mother let him
pick out his favorite. He chose raspberry crumb.

During the week his father said many
things, mostly with his hands. He rubbed
Palmer's hair and squeezed his shoulder and
tugged on his shirt and tickled his ribs and
pulled him backward with a finger hooked in
the back pocket of his jeans and lightly brushed
the side of his neck with his fingertips as he
stopped and chatted with friends. Each of these
things had a different meaning to Palmer and
yet the same—a language unlearned, of words
unheard, that came to roost at some warm and
waiting perch far below his ears.

He could not remember the last time his
father called him "big guy."

In other years his father had always stopped at the shooting gallery, where flat yellow ducks cruised smugly until shot in the eye: *pop ping . . . pop ping*. This year they walked by, not even looking. Palmer tried not to hear, but even as he bobbed on a merry-go-rounding horse, as he breathed deeply the sweet crispy tangle of a funnel cake, there it was: *pop ping*.

On Friday he rode his bike to the old train station. He heard them before he saw them, a noise like turkeys. He pulled up in front of the crates. The top crates towered high above him, and the whole slatted, gobbling tenement occupied more space than the boarded-up station. In the shade of the old ticket window a man sat whittling a stick.

"Better not stand there too long," the man called, laughing. "Smell'll knock ya over."

Palmer stayed a long while, his eyes closed, listening, trying to feel.

On Friday night the shooting gallery was mobbed. And at home the golden bird was gone from the mantel.

39

Until he found himself there, he had not been sure that he could come.

He had awakened with a start. He was sweating. His throat was sore. His dreams had been noise, the birdscream of thousands, a shrill wail that came on like day itself until his own voice was swept away with it.

The street was still in shadow, the grass in the park wet with dew. He first heard the shots as he trotted through the playground, past the sliding board where he had once rowdied with the guys. From the sound of the shots—*pop pop*—he might have thought the shooting gallery was ahead, except there were no *pings*.

Gunshot mixed with its memory in the picnic grove.

He was surprised at the size of the crowd already there. He had not before understood how early in the day one must begin in order to kill, and watch killed, five thousand birds by nightfall.

Someone, turning, saw him and bowed with a sweep of the hand. "Hey, looks like a wringer kid here. He musta got up late. Make way." Others turned, staring, smiling. He ran.

There was a grandstand, like at the Little League field. It was full. He stood beside it. Directly across the field from him the wringmaster in his neon pink baseball cap was directing the wringers.

Twice as high as the grandstand and almost as long was the mountain of crates housing the five thousand birds—four thousand and something now that the shooting had begun. A truck with an elevator platform lifted workmen to the top of the stack. Crates were emptied, five pigeons at a time, into two white wooden boxes, each about the size of Dorothy's bicycle basket.

While one box was on the field, the other was being reloaded with birds. Each box had five compartments, each compartment with a pigeon, a hatch and a string to open it.

The boxmaster wore an orange vest.

The shooters were to the left. They aimed their quarter-size black barrels toward the open end of the field. Here the sound was not *pop*. It was *boom*.

The waiting shooters chatted and joked with each other, their guns slung like baseball bats on their shoulders. But when a shooter stepped up to the white chalk line, he became all business. His face was grim, his eyes intense and focused on the white box ten feet in front of him. In this the shooters were all alike.

In other ways they differed. Some, when they stepped up to the line, shouldered the gun immediately and aimed at the box, as if this were a day to kill five thousand boxes. Others were more patient, holding the gun across their chest at parade rest until the first bird was released. A few shooters stood at attention, the heel of the gun resting on the ground.

There were differences among the pigeons as well. Some, when their hatch was raised, simply walked out, head bobbing, as if this were nothing more than a stroll on a city sidewalk. Others began at once to peck about for food. Others came out flying, although one, causing much laughter, flew only to the top of the box. Sooner or later most of them took off.

In Palmer's memory, recorded during his first visit to Pigeon Day six years before, the birds were shot out of the sky, above the treetops, among the clouds. He was surprised to find now that it did not really happen that way. In fact, the birds seldom flew more than shoulder-high to a man before a blast of pellets stopped them. They seemed not so much to be shot down as tripped. The men might as well have waited by the box and whacked them with a bat as they came out. The pigeons were denied even the elegance of a long fall.

Occasionally there was a stubborn bird that refused to fly. It would poke and peck about, perhaps circling the box, perhaps even ambling over to the spectators, who would laugh and shoo it back to the field. But the crowd's patience with stubborn birds was short. Soon they would be calling, "Toss 'im!" And the box-master would attempt to scoop up the bird in a long-handled fishing net and toss it into the air and run.

Boom.

If the boxmaster could not catch the bird, the scorekeeper would cry, "Fire!" and the shooter would.

Boom.

And sometimes the invisible pellets, like a sudden gust of wind, not only killed the uncooperative walking bird but kicked it into the air as well, as if to say, *There, you stubborn bird,* now *you're flying, aren't you?*

But shooters did not like to shoot a walker, because even a killed walker was worth no more than a wounded flyer—that is, one point in the scorekeeper's book. A killed flyer earned two points for the shooter, while a wounded walker scored a mere half point. Missing a flyer altogether was sure to bring a round of good-natured jeers from the spectators. But unluckiest of all was the shooter who completely missed a walker: he faced both a one-point deduction and a lifetime of ribbing.

Once every four or five boxfuls, a pigeon got away clean. Missed entirely by the buckshot, it flew over the reaching arms of the crowd and into the sky, circled the field several times and was gone.

On the table by the scorekeeper stood a golden bird, this year's Sharpshooter Award.

The wringers had learned their jobs well. At the feet of the pink-hatted wringmaster they crouched like sprinters, counting five shots. They sprang onto the field three at a time, one with a new, loaded box, the other two after downed pigeons. They did not wring the necks of the wounded in the field, for that would waste time, and the wringmaster was holding a stopwatch and calling the seconds. They dashed back with both living and dead swinging in their fists. Some held the birds by the neck, some by the feet. Some wringers wore wristbands.

The wringing was done on the sidelines, the dead birds dropped into large dark-green trash bags.

Palmer noticed that Beans, Mutto and Henry always worked as a threesome. Their turn came about every fifteen minutes. They never rotated jobs. Henry always did the boxes.

When the sun had cleared the tallest trees, Palmer felt a hand squeeze his little finger. It was Dorothy.

"Did you eat?" she said. "Your mother said you didn't eat breakfast."

"I'm not hungry," he said.

They both looked ahead, at the shooting field, as they spoke. Dorothy did not let go of his finger. With every boom of a shotgun he felt her flinch. At every neck wringing, she squeezed his finger. He could hear her breathing.

Though he had seen little of Dorothy since she returned from her vacation three weeks before, he was not surprised that she was beside him now, here.

Through most of the morning it had been a relief to Palmer to see that he was ignored by Beans and Mutto. Sometimes the pursuit of a flopper brought one of them within ten feet of where he stood, but they went about their business of snatch and dash and never seemed to notice him—until now. This time when Beans snatched a wounded bird flopping in the grass, instead of heading straight back to the wringmaster, he detoured over to Palmer. His teeth even yellower in the sun, his eyes wild with glee, he thrust the pigeon before Palmer's face, and then Dorothy's, and as he had so often pretended, wrung its neck. The bird's orange button eye blinked.

Dorothy's eyes were shut. She backed away. "I have to go."

Palmer caught her by the arm. "Wait."

They stood staring at each other's face, the only place their eyes were safe. Double-barreled booms and laughter mingled with smells of mustard and onions and barbecue and gunsmoke.

He could not wait any longer to ask. "Where did you let him go?"

"Nipper?" she said, as if she didn't know.

"Yeah. Where?"

"In the city."

Palmer was puzzled. "The city? I thought you went to the shore."

He had pictured Dorothy standing on a boardwalk or beach, tossing Nipper into the air, Nipper soaring over the sand, the foaming surf. He imagined a pigeon would have a good life at the seashore.

"We did," she said.

She was not making this easy.

"But you just said the city."

"We stopped off in the city"—a boom, she flinched—"for a day."

He remembered his trip to the city two years before, his delight in the pedestrian pigeons strolling, nodding up and down the sidewalks right along with the people. That too, now that he thought about it, seemed like a good life for a pigeon.

He nodded. "City, huh?"

She nodded.

"Did you, like, reach up and throw him into

215

the air and he flew away?" He wanted a clear picture to remember. "Or did you let him down on the sidewalk, and he walked along with the people?"

She twitched at a gun boom. She took a step back. "No, none of that. I rolled down the car window and he flew out."

It wasn't how Palmer would have wished. "While you were driving? Or stopped?"

"Stopped."

"In the traffic? Downtown? Where?" Still trying to picture it.

Another gun boom. She shivered as if it were December and not August. "At the railroad yards."

Railroad yards.

Palmer grabbed her by both arms and squeezed. "What?"

She squirmed. "What what?"

"Did you say railroad yards?"

"Yes. Stop it."

She twisted away from him and ran back through the people. Palmer caught her at the back of the crowd. He planted himself in front of her.

She sneered. "Treestumping again?"

"Dorothy"—he was screeching—"you let him out at the *railroad yards*."

Dorothy threw up her hands. "So?"

"*So?* The *railroad yards* are where they go to trap *pigeons* and bring them *here*. Why did you have to let him go *there?*"

A boom was followed by a second, louder explosion of cheers and howling laughter. Something outrageous had happened.

Dorothy stared, stunned, at Palmer. Her lips quivered. "*We* don't know about that stuff. Nobody ever told *us* that. Nobody in *my* family shoots pigeons!" She was screaming.

Heads turned. Dorothy ran off. This time Palmer did not follow.

40

He knows how it will end.

He can see it. His bird terrified in the smothering darkness of the box—it's like a coffin—when suddenly one wall springs up and light pours in and he's free to go. He steps out onto grass and feathers, thinking, Hey, where's the bedroom? He takes another step, looks around. There are people, people everywhere, more people than he has ever seen. But he is not afraid. The people he has known, the boy and the girl, were always good to him. He almost thinks of them as pigeons. He wonders if they—

The blast knocks him off his feet, drives him sideways, like the other blizzard long ago. There is pain in his wing. It drags. It will not move. He cannot stand straight or walk right. He tries to fly but labors only inches into the gray, sour cloud and flops back to earth. The people are noisy. The people are laughing and cheering and whistling. They are happy. He has never seen so many happy people. He wobbles toward them. He wants to be with them, with all those happy faces.

And then he sees that one face is different, one face is not laughing, is not happy. He knows the face. He would know it anywhere. Dragging his wing through the feathers that cover the ground, he heads for the face, he is limping toward the face when the second blast comes—

He whispered, "Nipper . . . Nipper . . ."

At the old train station on Friday, a swelling gobble of noise had come from the crates. Here they were silent. If Palmer had not known better, he would never have believed there were thousands of pigeons behind the wooden slats.

"Nipper . . . Nipper . . ."

He whispered into the crates. He stood on tiptoes and crawled on hands and knees, peering into the dark strips of space between the slats. Orange eyes flashed in the dark. He could not hope to reach the ones on top.

"Nipper . . ."

Nipper was here. He knew it. Somewhere in the canyon wall of crates towering above him.

Unless he was already shot.

"Nipper . . ."

"Hey, kid—"

A workman coming around the corner, pointing.

"Let's go. Move it. You can't be back here. Out with everybody else."

Palmer thrust a hand as far as it would go into one of the spaces. He wiggled his fingers, feeling only darkness.

The man was coming. "Kid—*now!*"

Summer has nearly two months to run, but the shooting field, covered in feathers, has a look of gray, demented autumn.

A man with a bamboo rake pulls shotgun shells into piles.

The mound of green plastic bags grows taller than the wringmaster's neon pink cap. Sometimes a bulge of plastic moves.

The line of shooters is never more than seven or eight deep, yet it never ends. The golden pigeon never blinks.

People point hot dogs at wounded, scurrying birds, yell to wringers, "There! There!"

The boxmaster makes a mistake. He opens two hatches at once. Out fly a pair of pigeons—

boom—knocked from the air with one shot. A double kill! A rare deuce! Four points! The crowd goes wild.

The biggest cheer of all goes to a yellow cat, which streaks onto the field, snatches a wounded bird and streaks off into the trees.

Gunsmoke and afternoon sunlight.

Someone tosses a Frisbee onto the field. The shooter on line fires. The Frisbee lurches and falls. A wringer dashes out, snatches the disc and pretends to strangle it. The wringmaster laughs. The crowd howls. The scorekeeper maintains a stern face, disqualifies the shooter.

People come and go, changing the composition but not the shape of the crowd.

Only Palmer stays through it all.

Sunsmoke.

Palmer cursed the sameness of the pigeons. Some of them had dark feathers—charcoal— and as they exploded on the ground and in the air, Palmer thanked them for so clearly not being Nipper.

But three out of four birds that walked out of the white box looked just like his: gunsmoke gray. Nipper had no special markings, nor had

Palmer ever thought to fix a band to his bird's leg or neck, for he knew without reading a book that of boys and pigeons, it is the boy who, so to speak, wears the collar, that it is never the pigeon, but the boy, who is lost.

Not knowing which gray-feathered bird might be Nipper, Palmer believed that every one was. Over and over, a thousand times, he was sure he saw Nipper killed. A thousand times he felt the sting of the buckshot. A thousand times he saw Nipper's neck wrung.

Occasionally a pigeon flapped into the air and stayed there, feathers intact, not only stayed there but rose higher and higher into the gray cloud, then above it, above the treetops, into the sky. A miracle! As the bird circled the field Palmer silently celebrated, his shoulders shrugging up and down in support of the wonderfully working, unshot wings. Around him people shot their fists at the sky and cursed. Others cheered the bird, toasted it with bottles of soda pop hoisted high. Still others jeered the not-so-sharpshooting shooter.

Eventually each miracle bird flew out of sight, and each time Palmer whispered, "Let it be Nipper." Then he would hear the next gunboom.

He would see wringers galloping through the featherfall. He would see the swollen plastic bags across the way, gorged on pigeon corpses, and for an unspeakable moment he would be inside, in a stinking muggery of limp necks and orange eyes dead as buttons, and he was sure that his bird was one of them. Fertilizer.

It did not occur to Palmer that he had not eaten all day until a crewcut little kid with a cup of grape water ice stood beside him. The little kid mimicked every gunboom by pointing a purple-stained forefinger and barking, "Pow! Pow!"

While an empty white box was being replaced by a loaded one, the little kid looked up at Palmer and said, "Are you a wringer?"

"Do I look like it?" Palmer replied, not wanting to be bothered and already not liking this kid.

The kid was untouched by Palmer's sarcasm. "How old are you?" he said.

"Twenty-five," said Palmer.

The dumb kid continued to stare up at Palmer as he slurped his water ice. "I'm seven.

"Hooray."

"In three years"—he held up three purple fingers—"I'm gonna be ten, and then—"

Boom

The first bird emerged from the freshly stocked white box, new shooter shooting.

The kid swung and pointed. "Pow! Pow!" And kept jabbering at Palmer. "And then I'll be—"

Boom

"Pow!—a wringer. I'm gonna wring their—" He tried to show what he would do but spilled purple slush over his own wrist.

Boom

"Pow! Pow! I'm gonna wring more than anybody. I'm gonna—"

Boom

"Pow! I'm gonna—"

Palmer was no longer hearing the yammering kid. He was looking up. The second pigeon out of the box had been another Nipper look-alike. It took a few casual steps and stopped to peck at the ground—a perfect target. Incredibly, the shooter had missed. The pigeon had taken off and was now higher than the afternoon sun. Another rare one, a miracle bird.

Blocking the sun with his fist, Palmer watched the bird circle the field, as the others had done. Palmer's shoulder muscles flexed to the rhythm of its wings, urging it on. It circled a fourth time. And again. It was not leaving. It was simply circling, circling. In fact, impossibly, *it seemed to be getting closer*.

It was Nipper.

Palmer simply and suddenly knew it.

And just as suddenly the horror of what he was doing struck him. For if Nipper truly was searching for him—and found him—

Palmer's own stupid, unthinking, upturned face was nothing more than bait luring his pigeon back to a second chance at death. This time the shooter would not miss.

Palmer covered his face with his hands. *No*, he prayed, *No No No.* . . .

Too late.

As the bird broke from its circle and began its long downward swing, the little kid beside Palmer pointed and screamed, "Look! It's coming back! It's coming back!" Palmer knocked the water ice from the kid's hand as the people began to look up. Fingers pointed, more faces turned. The shooter, who had been walking away, stopped and turned. His hand dipped into the pocket of his vest. The only sound was the outraged howl of the purple-plastered kid.

Palmer stepped away from the people then, into the clear, onto the shooting field, the better to be seen, for he knew now that there was no stopping it. Downward came the bird, lazily looping through the haze, gray in gray descending, gliding, a summer sledder down a slope of sunsmoke.

And landed on Palmer's head.

At that point even the howling kid shut up. His boggling eyes joined a townful of others aimed at a spot just above Palmer's forehead. Nipper's toes clutched and moved on his scalp, and for a strangely wonderful moment he felt himself crowned. The shooter was slipping shells into the twin barrels of his gun. And suddenly out of nowhere there was Beans, swiping at Palmer's head even as Nipper chuckled, sending the pigeon to the ground. Before Palmer could react, Beans was on the bird, scooping it up and sprinting to the center of the field. He hoisted the bird above his head and gave a long, ripping screech of triumph. He ran to the shooter, who stood stone-faced at the chalk line, shotgun at the ready. Mashing its wings, Beans shook the bird in the shooter's face. "It's yours! It came back! Kill! Kill!" He slammed the bird to the ground and ran for cover.

Palmer was running too. He saw the shooter shoulder his gun. His scream—"No!"—made a puff in the gunsmoke cloud. He splashed through the fallen feathers, which were deepest here in the territory between the shooter and the white box, like October leaves. He plunged facefirst, landing, sliding through the gray softness into his hobblywobbling bird. He pulled it into himself, curled himself around it, the comical, many-voiced, eight-toed friend blizzard-blown into his life one day. He closed his eyes and buried his face in the bed of feathers and waited for the shot. The *boom*.

He waited.

And waited.

And heard only silence.

He dared to lift his head and look around. The wringmaster was holding one arm out, making a gate behind which the wringers gaped. The wringmaster's other hand had Beans by the collar.

The shotgun stood on its heel at attention.

Palmer got to his feet. He ignored the blood-tacky feathers sticking to his face. He held Nipper close.

Standing there in feathers up to his sneaker knots, Palmer felt a peace, a lightness that he had never known before, as if restraining straps had snapped, setting him free to float upward. For a moment, feeling in his fingertips the quick beating of Nipper's acorn-size heart, he believed he could fly. Through a pigeon's eye he looked down from the sky upon the field, the thousands of upturned faces, and saw nothing at all to fear.

He reached out then, held his pigeon out to the people, slowly turned so they all could see, so they all would know.

Someone whistled.

Someone shouted, "Bang!" and laughter followed.

People booed.

Cradling his pigeon in both hands, Palmer walked from the field. The crowd parted just enough to let him through. He felt the cold stares of the people, he smelled the mustard on their breaths. A hand reached out. He flinched. It was a little hand, a child's hand, touching Nipper's wing, stroking it. A child's voice saying, "Can I have one too, Daddy?"

WAYMER—The annual Pigeon Day shoot held here on Saturday, was declared a rousing success by the event's organizers. More than 300 sharpshooters—"not all of them so sharp," quipped one official—took aim on some 5,000 birds released on the Memorial Park soccer field.

Proceeds from shoot entry fees, plus revenue from the weeklong Family Fest, netted the community almost $34,000 for maintaining its park.

An unexpected episode occurred during this year's event. At one point in the late afternoon an unidentified boy dashed onto the shooting field and retrieved a wounded pigeon. Shooting was immediately halted, and the reckless lad, perhaps seeking an unusual pet for himself, was allowed to leave the premises with the bird.

Certainly that lucky pigeon had not fallen under the aim of Howard Eckert. Eckert, 36, a dairyman from Harmony Farms, won this year's Sharpshooter's trophy as best marksman.

Said Eckert, "Anybody can hit a clay pigeon. These babies, you never know which way . . ."